SPLENDORS OF LOVE

SPLENDORS OF LOVE

JOHN B. THOMPSON

CUTTING EDGE

ISBN-13: 978-1-970848-04-5

Published by
Cutting Edge Books
PO Box 8212
Calabasas, CA 91372
www.cuttingedgebooks.com

CHAPTER ONE

F erris Macklin was luxuriating in her bath. It was one of the few luxuries she had and she was making the most of it. Ferris was, long and lithe and her skin had the golden transparency of a fat ripe peach. It was eggshell smooth and it excited easily when she'd caress it lightly or soap it. She was buried in a nest of lather and warm water with delightful points of herself peeking out occasionally. Her youthful breasts peeped through the snowy lather like cherry red peaks of a mountain breaking through a morning mist.

When Ferris bathed she let her mind run free. She thought of Unker Ben Macklin in whose home she and her father, Unker Ben's brother, lived. Unker Ben was old toothless, his skin hanging in folds and dew-laps and his memory wasn't what it used to be. Every morning, weather allowing he'd go to the lip of the high bluff in front of the house and say good mornin' to God with whom he tried to curry favor. His wife Sally had been dead thirty years but to the old man she was simply missing. He'd ask everyone he met if they'd met Sally. Of late he'd been somewhat annoyed with God because he never got any answer.

Ferris thought now as she almost always did about her first meeting with Bud Kitchen, member of a crooked and shiftless family of whiskey dealers and cattle rustlers. It had been on a swimming party to which the Kitchens' had not been invited, naturally. Her shyness manifesting itself, Ferris had dressed in a clump of bushes alone … She shuddered and hugged herself suddenly, the memory making sheets of revulsion and something that was not revulsion pour over her slender body. She'd come out of the creek and went to dress and when she was between bathing suit and clothes a bear-like figure stepped from the shadows and enveloped her deliciously nude body in an enveloping embrace. A rough palm prevented any outcry, although help was near then, she was borne to the ground with irresistable force and covered with the brutish hairy body. She tried to fight but some sort of weakening influence had enveloped her in a fog of paralysis.

"Ferris … Ferris … Ferris" came the passion thickened voice and his loose lipped mouth fled over her breasts to her mouth, forcing open and brutally attacking her tender lips. The overpowering maleness of him sent weakening shocking reaction over her. She knew the story of boy meets girl and she had romanticized it greatly but to her it was a subtle magnificent thing with almost holy overtones. This was a bruising hurtful animal sort of thing and it was this thought that gave her strength. Her precious treasure was going to be lost in the dark on a creek bank to a man who was more beast than man. She relaxed and let her head fall as though she'd fainted.

"Don't faint, Ferris," he begged in his low coarse voice. "You got to be awake, Ferris … I don't want you out …" He made the mistake of loosening his hand a little and she bit into it with all the incarnate savagery of a trapped tortured cat. He bawled hoarsely and, her mouth freed, Ferris screamed shrilly. He lumbered to his feet and disappeared in the brush. Ferris never thought of the rest of it because it was almost as unpleasant as the attack, without relieving features. She rolled sinuously in the tub and sat up angrily. It was always like this. She hated the thought but she would always let her mind dwell on it, then she'd go into a sensual trance as though she might have wished it to happen.

She hugged herself again, her taut water slicked breasts, leaped upward and outward from the pressure of her forearms. She looked down at them, cupped them gently and crooned, "I'm so sorry ... I'm so sorry".

Two men, strangers, obviously, dismounted from the Silver Bullet when it stopped in Tide Mississppi, just in time to nearly get blown away by a tornado. Glass and debris, road and store signs sucked into the vortex sped in the wake of the whirling black cloud. A deluge of rain followed the murderous twister that had ripped through the poor white and colored section and left it in shambles. On Main street, the mayor, Charlie Olsen a portly, nerveless man soon had emergency crews operating and rigged up a jury fire wagon, the other having wrecked and pinned the driver beneath it.

Ronald and Berry Summerville, brothers and strangers to Tide rescued their luggage from the flood waters, found a very light colored Negro who owned a car of sorts to use as a taxi. Berry, the elder brother, seeking early friends paid the boy on the spot and paid him generously.

He fingered the money and looked embarrassed. "That's certainly white of you Mr...."

"Summerville," said Ronald, "and he deserves no credit for being white. Both his parents were white."

The colored boy muffled a laugh with a palm. "That's rather well put."

"I think I read it some place. Go ahead and get the heap."

It was a fairly serviceable Ford of uncertain vintage since most of the identifying accessories had been either battered beyond recognition or replaced by various other parts of roughly the same fit. The engine was good and seemed to have no particular quirks.

"The two big trunks we'll put under the cootershell, Mr. Berry." He raised the trunk lid. "The bags can go in the back."

"Is that a cootershell?" asked Ronald.

"Yes sir. Colloquialism for turtleshell. A cooter is a turtle".

"I learn something every day. What is your name?"

"John Howard Patterson ... Junior."

"You're a handy guy to have around John. What do you do?"

"I taught a year but the strain of trying to teach children what their parents should have taught them in addition to their academic necessities seemed a little more than I could pull. A matter of temperament probably. I do odd jobs. I'm a fair gardner, a good cook, I can drive, clean house, wash and iron clothes. I'm as you say ... handy." There was a bitterness in his voice that they could understand.

They finished loading and got in. John turned around and headed out of town skirting the storm area then took a graveled road leading northwest.

"Say," said Berry sitting up suddenly. "Where're you taking us? I didn't tell you where we wanted to go."

John performed an attractive smile. His teeth were large, regular and white. "I guess everybody around here knows you brought Little River. When I heard your name I knew where you wanted to go."

"I suppose the house is finished and loaded."

"Yes sir. Mr. Hornsby finished it last week and Mrs. Hornsby decorated it ... I guess she's through. It's sure a slick house Mr. Berry."

"From what it cost it should be. The architect's fee would have built a fair house."

Ronald was nettled. "What the hell is all this? You snatch me up by the stacking swivel and yank me out to this ... this place where twisters drive splinters through skulls and tear down towns and electrocute bony old women ... and all the time I'm in a fog ... Is this some idea of yours that will drive the demon from me and make me a placid ..."

"Oh shut up" said Berry. "You said you wanted to go off on a South Sea Island and eat cocoanuts and such gunk ... be a hermit and commune with nature.

CHAPTER TWO

During World War II Ronald had been an infantry captain and came home with medals and honors. Being a little ancient for the Korean conflict, he answered the call of restlessness and became a correspondent, since his occupation was that of a writer of boisterous adventure tales that sold wildly, were made into pictures and were reprinted in the millions. His women were uniformly lovely, redheaded, black headed, tawny headed, blond and various shades of each. They were lusty, and voluptuous and their morals were highly adaptable ... especially to his heroes who were rugged, handsome and not a little brutal. The women, however, never seemed to mind being cuffed around because they seemed to sense that it was merely a normal prelude to greater things ... most of which were accomplished in bed but not boringly consistent on that point. His heroes were no sticklers for time and place and once love in the more intense shades had been made high over the earth while a plane out of control dipped and spun crazily until such time as love was served and the sure hand of the pilot could be spared for such non-essentials as piloting.

In Korea, Ronald began to lose weight. His nerves began to knot up and his stomach tortured him continuously. Ronald Summerville, erstwhile hero fled from a Chinese attack (although he was in no particular danger), screaming, left his material and gear and continued to flee until exhaustion chopped him down unconscious, mercifully near an aid station. When he recovered consciousness he was in a hospital in Tokyo a prey to acrid memories of his cowardly flight. He did have enough balance to see that it would be foolish in his state, at that time, to attempt to return … to possibly greater demonstrations of funk. So he came home.

In Toledo he went to the home of his brother, his sole living relative, excepting Tommy, Berry's son, who was away at school.

The road tilted sharply and they seemed to be climbing a ridge. Looking back he could see the red bed of the winding road, the verdant green valley and knew they were there. They leveled off at the top of the ridge and wound through dreamy deep woods of pine and hardwood.

They topped another rise, a small one this time and pulled left over a cattle gap made of old steel rails. Obviously this was a private road, narrow but graveled and well graded, and led winding through an archway of straight tall pines. Ronald leaned back and breathed deeply. The smells were like a breath of fragrant ether and acted on him like a hypnotic. Without intending to he relaxed and had to be shaken awake a few minutes later.

"Okay, Ron. Pile out."

"A pox on you for waking me from my dreams."

"We got to look the place over before night and figure on some supper. How do you like it?"

They got out and looked at the house, a modern dream of a house that nestled comfortably in a grove of gigantic trees. Elm, oak, pine, beech formed the armored guard. Troops of crabapple, wild plum, peach and pear kept the air alive with heady barrages of fresh aromatic fragrance.

"The only trouble about this" breathed Ronald wonderingly, "is that it's hard to believe."

"I thought maybe you'd like it" said Berry placidly. "John will you see to the dumping of that gear? You can bring in the bags. Just leave the trunks and I'll help you with them after a while. I got to take a look at the inside."

"You go ahead" said Ronald shoving his hands deep into his pants pockets. "I want to walk around and look at things."

He stared at the house, its woodsy setting and tried to finger the key to the harmony they enjoyed. The house was functional to a degree. He chuckled to himself. So were the trees. Two functional designs, regardless of humanity's opinion on the subject should be in harmony.

The house was of stone. Flat light brown stone thrown into a mass without too much attention to geometricity. The roof was without a true hip and seemed broken where it dipped supported by huge cypress beams forming a front veranda.

He was a man no longer but a sprite following the shadows as they leaped across declevities sucking in the opiate of spring in the forest.

Ronald sat erect suddenly. In the woods to his left came a crisp clear song. Rhythmic, repetitive but something that he had never heard or anticipated hearing. It gripped him and made a tightness in his chest, tensed his mucles and taunted his brain. What was it?

He was afraid to call John and ask him what it was. It might stop. If it did it might never repeat this song. The answer to the fear came in another song, exactly the same that started a little further away to his right. Just as clear but sweeter for the intervening distance. Then another still further, and a fourth directly behind the house until it seemed that they were a chorus spaced exactly right for their woodland symphony. He whipped out a tiny notebook that he kept to jot down thoughts and impressions, and tried to put the song into discriptive words. It was impossible.

"Chuck-*wills*-a-*widow,* chuck-*wills*-a-*widow.*" The words were plain enough but how to get the rhythm the smacking lisp of the *chuck* which was a prelude for the short refrain, the whistling whip to the rest of it? He put the book away and sat listening until he realized that darkness had set in. Then, there were other things to notice. Fireflies had turned on the stage lighting for the symphony and bobbed about like fairies trying to find their way through a mystic forest peopled by giants that were trees and witches that were underbrush.

"Soup's on" called Berry from the front door and Ronald almost cursed him. He got up and got his first look at the front of the house. It was almost solid glass, louvered so that when open it was almost out of doors. It was cozily lighted, like a crystal coronet set on the brow of the ridge.

He went into the tremendous living room and let the richness of it flow into his senses.

"Hey, want your eggs to get cold?"

He walked through the double doors into a kitchen and dining room combined that was nearly as big as the living room with the stove, refrigerator, sink and innumerable shelves and drawers in the exact center of the room. About the walls were booths, a huge natural wood table with comfortable chairs and on it was a quick feast.

"Who's the cook ... not you surely."

John came to the table with a huge coffee pot which advertised its newness by its chromium glare. "The handy man again, sir. I hope the eggs don't hurt your stomach. I scrambled them in butter with a fragment of onion, cream, mushrooms and just a suggestion of Parmesian cheese."

Ronald look at him. "No handy man cooks like that now, Johnny. Where did you chef?"

The smile seemed to light up the room. "Cooking, sir, is an imaginative art. The reason recipes always seem to flop is because if they were written by a good cook he had forgotten just what amounts of everything he used and the recipe was a snatch at memory ... usually off the beam by some distance. I use recipes as a reminder. I never follow one slavishly."

Berry chuckled. "Have some ham."

"Country cured," added John.

"How do you know?" asked Ronald, "What distinguishes country cured ham from any other?"

"Take the first taste which will be better than a hundred words." He slid a thick ham steak off the platter onto Ronald's plate.

Ronald tasted and nodded. "I see what you mean ... Damn I'm hungry."

"Careful," said Berry. "Remember your stomach."

Ronald grunted and continued eating.

After supper he went back to the seat under the tree and communed with the sort of night he had not known since his days on T'Aau in the Pacific. Berry remained inside and looked about the kitchen with its cypress beamed ceiling, colorful appointments and spotless range and utensils.

"What do you think of this kitchen, Johnny?"

"I'm afraid I'm a little staggered. It's a dream kitchen ... I've been hoping I'd get a look at this house. I've heard so much about it. Wait till I tell people I cooked your first meal."

Berry lit a cigarette and patted his full stomach. The taste of the pungent spicy ham lingered on the back of his tongue as did the coffee that he did not like because it was too strong, but the after flavor was rich and complimented the smoke from his cigarette. "Didn't like that handy man handle too much did you?"

"Hardly that, sir. It's just that I have an education and it would appear that I'm wasting good training."

"No argument there but I think you know what you're up against here."

"Better than most. I sound bitter at times and I suppose at times I am but I'll never leave here."

"Why?"

"Because I've seen what it's like in the so called land of opportunity. I doubt that the South combined could muster a pest hole like Harlem or provide a race riot like Detroit. I'm constitutionally unsuited to teaching and I don't like digging ditches."

"All right, what do you see for yourself?"

John sighed. "To be frank, I think my optimism always keeps me looking for Santa Claus."

Berry nodded. "You manage to eat somehow."

"People in the south usually manage to eat. When I serve at the homes of the great on special occasions … cocktail parties and the like. I eat there and always take some home. Cumsha as it were. It's expected. All servants do it. Something tells me you're working up to something."

"I am. You're a sharp lad. What is your opinion of my brother?"

"I have none as yet. Some impressions maybe that might or might not be correct."

"He's been in a bad way and I'll have to watch him … maybe for a long time. He doesn't give any trouble but he gets moody and begins to feel world injustices, things like that. Then no one knows what will happen. I could go on for a long time and tell you a long story but I'm working up to an offer of employment slowly because I don't want to be refused."

John leaned against the stainless steel sink and shook with silent laughter. "You didn't want to rush me for fear I'd refuse and I didn't rush you for fear you might have someone coming from up north. We're a great pair of fencers."

"Then you'll stay?"

John nodded. "Somehow I don't feel that working for you in this capacity will place me ... I'm saying that badly. What I mean is, I don't think being a menial here will be quite the same as elsewhere. To begin with, you feel that you need me, therefore I have a service for hire ... not just a chow pusher to sling hash but a man with some conception of the artistic side of cookery ..." He looked at Berry squarely. "I could come in handy as a friend."

"When it comes to that" said Berry slowly, "I'd say you already have. You've got yourself a job. Need any help?"

"Yes sir, if I can have it. I despise to wash dishes and make beds. I could find someone to do that. I love to garden and cut grass and cook ... especially for parties and things like that but the drudge of the aftermath scares me."

"Get your help, as much as you need and I might say that you will be paid ... not as a hash slinger but as the head of my kitchen staff and general major domo."

The ready smile came again. "Like I said, working here will hardly be menial labor. Shall I stay on the premises?"

"By all means; that's what the cottage is out back for ... and what about your help?"

"I have a sister, rather a lovely girl I think, young, strong and hard headed. She'll be good for the job and we work as a team. We could stay together in the cottage."

"Why isn't she in school?"

"Hard headed, like I said. We've never discovered whether she actually doesn't want to go to school or because there are twelve in the family, she doesn't feel she should go when there are younger ones whom the education would benefit more. She and I are in the same boat. What could she do but teach school?"

"She doesn't like teaching?"

"She's too much like me. She doesn't like the idea. She has a high school education and she's very alert and sensible".

There was another silence when Berry said. "About your sister ... you don't think bringing her here might set up some complications?"

"What sort of complications?"

Berry shrugged and a frown corrugated the skin of his usually smooth forehead. "Hell, how do I know? Maybe I don't know what I'm talking about myself."

John stopped washing and half turned. "Complications of the sort you mean are all over. Frankly, I want to get her out of Tide before I have to kill someone."

"That bad?"

"She had to quit working for the Hodge family because she was a pick-up target from the time she left the house all the way to her job and the same thing in the afternoon. There is a family three miles from town ... name of Kitchen who are pretty tough on Negroes and they've been getting ugly when she refuses to have anything to do with them. There have been rumors that they might take her by force and that I'd hate to see. I know I'm in an unfavorable spot but there are some things I can't take."

"Aren't you a little optimistic, Johnny? Ronald is not predictable ..." He stopped and a rueful grin touched his face. "I'm not very predictable either. I'm not trying to make a prophecy but I'd hate for anything to happen that'd make you leave us".

John turned completely around. "Mr. Berry would you attack my sister?"

Berry turned red. "Good God ... no!"

The smile came on again. "Would Mr. Ronald?"

"Oh ..." Berry made a quick savage gesture with his left hand. "That isn't what I mean at all, Johnny."

"Then we have no problem. She is no better than any average healthy lovely youngster and I'm not trying to make it sound like she's the Madonna reincarnated. I'm not even certain that she's a virgin. I do know this, if she isn't then the act was a premeditated deliberate thing which she made right with herself before she made the first move. My point is this. I don't want her loused up by force by just any man who wants to drag her into the brush. I want her own desires to indicate what shall be done. In this day and time I think that even white people have the very same thing to contend with. There was an awful stink raised here not six months ago because a son of one the great ... Mr. Pearson's son to be pointedly nasty, took one of the neighboring farmer's daughters out, just a kid about sixteen but full of good flesh and probably loaded with the usual come hither quotient. Well, young Pearson took her out and when time came to say no she found him quite deaf and the struggle ended with the destruction of her maidenly virtue. The resultant turmoil was quite steamy with two brothers promising to shoot young Pearson on sight."

Berry chuckled. "No shotgun wedding?"

John shook his head. "No. I think that with certain meager exceptions most stratas have come to a belated awakening and see that such things only compound a bad situation and the sense of face gained is felt only by parents in most cases. Youth has its own way of caring for such things. It appears that the James family though deep water Baptists are quite direct in their thinking.

Young Pearson is away at school, the girl did not get with child. She graduated with her class without being sneered at and seems to have suffered little harm."

"Sex" said Berry without originality, "is here to stay".

"So," John continued, "as long as my sister is not physically harmed and forced into an act, what she does we must leave in her hands. Such is the way things are now".

CHAPTER THREE

Ronald sat on the edge and hung his feet over swinging them like a small boy, feeling a greater peace than he could ever remember. He thought of the treachery of Madelyn but the ache was distant and hardly felt at all. She hadn't wanted him to go when all the time she was one of the many reasons why he had taken the job as correspondent. Madelyn was not the sort of woman a writer should have married because there must be nothing before her. Ronald was not a hack but a man who wrote when the spirit was upon him and if that occasion interfered with her schedule then no writing was done. One magazine refused to consider his serial because once they had to omit an installment because Madelyn had decided that a trip to a dog show was more important. He had hoped that absence might make some change in her and it had. She had taken to drink and to anyone that had the male look. Once it was only a male look which subsequently proved to be female with a distinctly unfemale attitude. It had been talked about in some detail so when he began to be the recipient of pitying looks and whispers went behind hands he was clever enough to guess the rest. There had been the inevitable scene … triangular, of course, with one Braxton Semple, a sort of man about town and comforter of women whose husbands' business absences often caused sorrow and loneliness. He had given Semple a rather energetic beating, saving one last effort for Madelyn, a kick that sent her sprawling on the floor. He stood over her and dared her to either whimper or make a sound. He also left a very potent threat behind him when he took his leave.

He picked her up and flung her into a deep chair. He was trembling with rage and nervousness, his fingers clenching and opening spasmodically, his eyes red and flaming, his teeth bared like a hunting animal. Madelyn, who read newspapers could see the headlines. "Prominent Matron and Friend, Victims in Double Killing."

She was frightened half out of her wits and sank back in the chair wondering why she had had the apartment sound proofed now that a scream might save her life. Braxton Semple was a bloody hulk on the rug and might even now be drawing his last breath.

"I have a few words to say", he said. He did not sound like Ronald, he sounded like a murderer about to commit, a sadist playing with his victim. Her bones seemed turned to water.

"I'm pulling out of this joint and I'm going to Toledo. *If* in six months you haven't gotten a divorce … I don't care where or how, I'll come back here and finish what I started today. If you think I'm just blowing because I like the wind in my hair … *just try me*".

He walked out and in four months was a free man. Free! He laughed grimly. Could it be called freedom?

The sweet music of the bird back of the house stopped and let him listen to the *wills-a-widows* farther away. Farther and farther until they died to a mere whisper. His blood tingled and he took several deep breaths. He felt like he was sinking … sinking … then came the blood-freezing certainty that he was. With a wild lunge he rammed both feet into the sliding earth and dived out into the black night like a flying squirrel. Instinctively, he had tried for the treetops rather than fall seventy or eighty feet almost straight down to certain injury if not death.

He struck a slim young pine breast on and snapped it off, feeling a million tingles as the needles struck through his clothes, struck another then grasping wildly hung onto a third. It bent gracefully over depositing him on the soft carpeted earth with scarcely a jar. He sat down and wiped the bitter sweat of horror from his face. Diving headlong into the darkness ... sitting like a fool on the edge of the bluff and letting it cave off with him. His skin prickled maddeningly where pine needles had pricked him but otherwise he was unhurt.

He got up and walked back until he came to the foot of the bluff. He was appalled at the distance he had covered by his terrific spring but it was the only thing that had saved him from serious injury or worse.

He looked up, just able to make out the dim outlines of the edge and the scallop he had taken out where the cave-off had sent him soaring into the night.

A low rattling growl sounded almost at his feet and a yelp of fear strained itself through stiff lips. The animal crashed off through the undergrowth and he could envision a catamount ... or whatever the horrible wildcats were called, slinking away to get a better vantage and spring on his back. Like a squirrel he ran up the sloping face of the rise until it became sheer, then stopped, his heart pounding wildly. He looked back into the black void, his ears producing all sorts of weird suggestions to his leaping nerves. Slowly and with infinite care, he continued up the face of the bluff, utilizing almost non-existent hand and footholds, roots and starved scrubby bushes. One root, feeling cold and damp from the dew made him gasp and start because it felt like a snake. He fell some six feet before another bush stopped his plunge and he hung there for a long time weak and sweating before he could begin climbing again.

When finally he dragged his drenched body over the edge and felt the grass beneath his fingers he stretched out and listened to his heart bang around in his chest like a berserk basketball player trying to dribble a hole in the floor.

He was covered with red clay that turned to mud when mixed with his sweat. He was exhausted and had gone through another of his cowardly spells. He'd have fled madly but he was not supplied with wings so the race had been a slow one. The urge, however had not been wanting.

Fifteen minutes later he felt like trying to make it to the house so he got up weakly and walked across the lawn.

Berry was at the piano when he entered, teasing half-hearted melodies from the big grand, soft nostalgic things that did not seem to have much object, just lazily floating away from the keys; half of this song, a refrain from another ... and Ronald felt an urge to cry.

"Holy mackerel!" Berry was turned on the piano bench looking at his brother with incredulous eyes.

"All right ... so I fell off the bluff".

"Fell off?"

"Well, yes and no".

"Yes and no"? echoed Berry, stifling a desire to burst into a laughter. "What sort of talk is that?"

"It seems that a piece of earth gave way where I was sitting. I just escaped breaking my neck. I'm going home tomorrow."

"Home where?"

Ronald was stumped for a moment. "I'll build me one. I'll build it where the hazards to life and limb are less".

"You're a dunce. Are you hurt?"

"Now you ask".

"Well are you?"

"No ... and no thanks to that damn booby trap on a bluff. My own agility and hardiness saved me."

"Mind if I laugh ... now that it seems you're not hurt?"

"Go ahead. Please do me the courtesy to wait until I'm in the bath before you get too noisy with it". Ronald walked stiffly away and Berry leaned on the piano and shuddered with mirth.

"What happened," asked John standing in the doorway to the kitchen.

Berry wiped his eyes. "It seems that Ronald was sitting on the edge of the drop out there and it caved off with him. I gather that by a dint of fast footwork and a little flying he managed to get by with a few scratches and nothing more. He's going to leave the country and build himself a house some place where there are fewer hazards ... like caving bluffs and such".

"Will he?"

"No! He'll have forgotten about it in the morning. Right now he looks like a bull had wallowed him around in red mud and he's mad as a wet hen."

"I'm through now", said John wiping his hands on a dish towel. "I've looked over the supplies and it seems that Mrs. Hornsby did all right by that end. I'll go in tonight and bring Mart back with me in the morning. She can look over the linens and household things and see if anything is needed. Off hand I'd say no. The Hornsbys are thorough people. Nice people, by the way. Did you ever meet them?"

"Once. I brought my plans down and engaged him to build the house and her to decorate it. I didn't want to be bothered with details. So far I have no complaints. This place took my eye as soon as I saw it."

"Did you buy the whole place?"

"Yes".

"What will you do with a thousand acres?"

Berry sighed and leaned back. "Haven't decided. May raise pine trees."

John chuckled. "You've a good stand of them now".

"Your sister's name is Mart?"

"Martha but somewhere it got shortened". His face grew serious. "Mart's a good kid. Mr. Berry, but ..." He shrugged in a sort of hopeless way. "I guess you'd say she's too good looking. Trouble dogs her steps and she stays home too much. I sure hope this works out because it'll mean a lot to her. What I mean is, I hope she won't complicate anything ... like you were talking about".

Berry got up and walked to the glass wall and stood looking out. "Johnny, boy, you're working for a couple of sprung timbers. Both of us have had a lot of knocks. Maybe we'll relax with a crash and start feeling our manhood again. Maybe we won't tame it and will get worse. I don't know anything anymore but you can take it from me this is a last effort. I stayed around in Toledo after my wife died and made money but I hated the place and when I could find a good excuse I got the hell away from there. Ronald was my excuse. We came here either to duck what we couldn't beat or to see if in a new and kinder atmosphere we couldn't lick it. It'll all come out and you'll have a good picture of it eventually. If the kid is beautiful maybe she will complicate things because although we were born and reared to young manhood in Tennessee we don't hold with this inferior race business. Maybe she'll throw a fast hook into one of us. Maybe we'll only think of her as decorative and have a good healthy affection for her. Who knows what'll happen? We can't duck things forever, though. Wherever we go there'll be something that will have some disturbing potential". Berry muttered a curse and turned around. "Do I sound as silly to you as I do to me?"

"Not particularly. You have a sensitive mans appreciation for the possible ... and probable".

Berry's eyes narrowed. "Why do you say probable?"

"You weren't speaking in terms of possibility. It is the probability that has you worried. I know what you mean about sounding silly. You feel you're becoming concerned before any necessity arises. Like a man wearing a raincoat on a sunshiny day just in case it rains".

"Exactly ... but maybe that'll give you some insight into the situation. Johnny, we're both pretty scared of fire ... like any child freshly burnt. Mine isn't fresh but it's there just the same. It's bad when a man overloads himself with responsibility".

"Like how, sir?"

"Like feeling such confidence in a doctor that you lose sight of his training and let him putter around while your wife dies with cancer".

Berry looked blindly out at the blackness. "Confidence can't take the place of knowledge ... especially someone else's knowledge. He wanted her seen by a specialist but I had confidence ... and she died. I think some of me died with her".

John said nothing and there was a long silence but Berry did not feel it an uncomfortable one. He sensed a depth of understanding that rose above the spoken word. "I'll see you early in the morning," said John softly.

Sure ...".

Berry sat at the piano struck one chord. He got up and turned all the lights out except a faint glow of blue indirect fluorescent tubes along the edge of the ceiling and took a chair where he could look out across the dark void of the valley. It always pained him to think of what might have been and tonight it was particularly bad.

"Got your laugh out" asked Ronald as he came out fresh in T shirt and white drill trousers.

"Yeah".

Ronald sat down and lit a cigarette. "Got you again?"

"In a way. Got wound up in something with Johnny and it sort of drifted up to the surface."

"What sort of something"?

"His sister's coming to help with the house".

"What's wrong with that?"

"Johnny thinks she's beautiful. She probably is and I got to wondering what sort of an effect she'd have on us".

"That was presumptuous of you".

"It was nuts but we got to talking about it anyway. There are some men in Tide who don't take no for an answer and she's afraid of trouble. Young, lovely, Negro women aren't treated the best down here by white men unless they're rich men's darlings or selling it ... then of course they're treated like all sellers of bodies".

"So she's coming here to be safe and to disrupt the even tenor of our lives. Sometimes I think you're the one who's nuts".

"I admitted it. I don't know why I feel about her coming here like I do".

Ronald grinned. "Maybe you are having visions. Another Nostradamus. I'd like to know when this vision struck you. If you'll recall I've been dragged along by the nose in this deal without knowing why when or where".

"I thought it best that way".

"What about your business?"

"I sold it".

"In heaven's name, why?"

"Because you needed a keeper".

"Look, I know I'm all busted up inside and all that. I know I've got a streak a mile wide and I know I've acted pretty wacky on occasion. I know that if I don't straighten out I'm likely to crack up but is that any reason for you to chuck everything and become a nursemaid?"

A ponderous frown grew on Berry's brow. "Sit still and listen to me for a moment then I don't want to hear another word about it. I haven't mentioned it before because it is something I don't talk about ordinarily. Remember when Betty died?"

"I sure do. I was in Hollywood at the time …"

"That's right you were. Making kale hand over fist but when she died what did you do? You came to Toledo, chucked the job because they wouldn't hold it over for you. I'll never forget the day you came into the living room where I sat with a big red ball of agony surrounding me. You said Okay boy, I'm here. Forget the footwork and details. I got everything in hand.' "

"From then on I did exactly nothing but wander around and let you do it. That trouble came up in the business where I had stripped my part to the bone and it had to be put back. You used thirty thousand of your own money to pick up the pieces and underwrote a hundred thousand in case they didn't fit right. For that you got your money back and a measly block of stock. No interest, nothing. All right. You go to Korea and come back a little frayed at the edges. I'm sick of Toledo and anything that reminds me of Betty. The company has prospered and I have money in the bank. I sold my interest and retained a good healthy block of shares in Tommy's name. I was ready to quit anyhow and this was it. I came here to look out for you because of the guy that stepped into the living room that day and said, Okay boy, I'm here.' That's the story and I'm *here*. You're here and you'll stay here until you crack or get well. I don't want to hear another damn word on the subject and I mean from now on. *Get it?*"

For a moment Ronald was afraid of his hulking brother, sitting tense and belligerent in his chair. Then he understood. "Okay, Berry. Not another word. I guess you'd kick me good if I mentioned it again".

"Nope. I've done better than that".

"Like what?"

"Think it over and maybe it'll come to you. I'm going to drink a pint of whiskey and go to bed."

"I'm going to bed without the whiskey".

The bedroom smelled of newness but the sheets had been laundered and smelled of cedar. Ronald snuggled cozily in bed letting the peace of the night steal into his system. Outside he could still hear the grand opera of the woodsy night and the breeze that came through the open window was almost a fluid, cool and gentle.

Madelyn came into his thoughts bringing back the old ache, the need for close companionship, the need for affection and love, the need for the soft skin of a lovely woman beneath his fingertips, the need for the cleansing action of towering passion to ease and calm him. But no Madelyn. Her beauty offended him now and the memory of how she had made of her body a sordid thing of pure sensation without even the observance of good taste revolted him and it lost much of its attraction. The ache was not because of Madelyn. Rather because of the emptiness her absence provided. Ronald was a sentimentalist, a dreamer, a man who needed love like other men need food. Without it he was only half a man. He made a wry face. At the moment he felt like an even smaller fraction what with his state of mind, the nervous fear which he masochistically preferred to label cowardice and general confusion that seemed to cling to him like an annoying blanket of thin fog.

Sleep came as it had come in the car earlier that day, like calm warm water flowing over smooth sand.

CHAPTER FOUR

He bounced out of bed and looked out on the early evidence of a new day. It was still dark but in the east there was a faint lighting of the sky, a pale blue streak that formed a perfect backdrop for the sawtoothed pine studded horizon. He dressed hurriedly and walked quietly out of the house, across the grassy sward to the edge of the bluff where he watched the virgin day begin its life.

He was relaxed and so hypnotized by the crystal purity of the world in the morning sun that he lost track of time and wandered further than he had intended. Suddenly he came out into clearing at the back of which was a grey old house with a steep roof and a wide front porch. The ubiquitous trees were dotted about without order showing that they antedated the house. Then he realized he was being watched and turned, suffering a slight shock at what he saw.

An old man who had once been tall but was now bent and as spare as a crane, dressed in ancient black alpaca with a droopy string tie and spotless white shirt. His hair was white and sparse and his eyes burned from deep sockets.

The toothless ancient shambled toward him, his mouth half open and his eyes fixed on Ronald's.

"Good morning," said Ronald with something akin to alarm, but the old man came on until he was quite close then he stopped, his gaze as fixed as ever.

"You seen Sally"? he asked in a cracked senile voice, his face anxious and his manner intensely eager.

"No ... I don't suppose I have. I just came here yesterday. We ... my brother and I live in the new house ..." He stopped and gestured vaguely. The old man obviously cared little about such details.

Hope died slowly from his face and he shook his head. "Beats all. *Nobody* ain't seen her".

"Who is Sally? Maybe I could keep a look out for her".

"Sally? Why she's the purtiest critter in these here parts ... Lost her some time back ..." Despair etched itself into the wrinkles about the toothless mouth. "I'm goin' a' die one day and I sure would like to see her again before I does. Come out here ever' morning to sort of have a talk with God about it but I must of been a bad sinner in my day. He won't help me none". The old man turned and walked away talking to himself. "Watches all the time for sparrows to fall and such triflin' things like that. Can't seem to get no sense ..." The voice waned and Ronald could hear no more.

He was taut and nervous from the old man's speech and appearance. He certainly offered no physical threat but Ronald felt an almost overpowering desire to run. He clenched his teeth and muttered a curse, almost crying out at the sudden appearance of a slip of a girl. She was dressed in a simple green cotton dress and wore ragged moccasins on her feet. She stopped as she saw him.

"Oh ... I reckon it was you talking with Unker Ben. I hope you didn't pay him any mind".

Ronald was a little staggered. Never in all his life had he seen such an extraordinary woman. Her hair, her eyes were nearly the same color, the eyes a little lighter. They were a soft melting grey, her hair, darker, was black and yet not black. The lightest black he ever had seen. It was so fine he knew she'd never make it behave well. He strove to find a word for it and failed. Her skin was so smooth and youthful that he swallowed seeming to taste a vague reflection of it on his palate. It was tanned faintly and touched with rose. Her lips, curved with breathtaking grace, full but not thick and gave the impression of melting tenderness, mobile and sensitive. Under his frozen scrutiny she flushed, the wave of blood dying her skin as though it was translucent.

"I'm sorry", he said blushing also. "I didn't mean to stare. That was Uncle Ben?"

"Yes sir. He's a little funny".

"So I thought. It appears that he's anxious about someone named Sally."

"Yes sir. He comes out to the bluff every morning to speak to God about her. She was his wife and she died nearly thirty years ago."

Ronald flexed his fingers only then realizing that his fists had been clenched tightly and his palms were slick with sweat.

"Yes, he must be a little funny".

"Oh, he's not any trouble, not crazy or anything like that. He's just a little touched about Sally. He doesn't have much memory left, but he remembers her. Daddy says she looked a lot like me".

"I'm Ronald Summerville," he said tentatively.

Her smile was quick and brilliant. "I'm Ferris Macklin I think we're neighbors."

"Yes. We just got in yesterday afternoon … just in time to see the cyclone strike Tide."

Her face shadowed. "It must have been terrible. Two men electrocuted, an old woman killed by lightning, several Negroes and three white people killed by the wind".

"Have you seen our house?"

"Oh yes". Her eyes became ecstatic. "I was over there nearly every day while they were building it and I helped Mrs. Hornsby some while she was decorating it".

"You don't speak like one of the indigenous natives, Ferris. You speak like you've had education".

She smiled again and he noticed a shallow dimple flash into view briefly. "My father was a professor at the University. All my schooling has been under him. He's Unker Ben's brother".

"He doesn't teach any more?"

"No sir". Her face clouded. "I think there was some trouble up there and we had to come live with Unker Ben. That's been a long time ago".

"I suppose I'd better be getting back" he said lamely, hating himself for forcing an unpleasant subject. "They'll be waiting breakfast for me".

She smiled again and the sight of it dug into his vitals. "I'll have to get back too or Unker Ben will be hollering for me".

"Will I see you again ... I mean why don't you ..." He could hardly ask her over to the house with no one there but two men. Then he remembered that John's sister was coming. "Why don't you come over some time. My brother plays the piano beautifully".

She nodded vigorously. "I'd like to, sir. I play a little myself".

"That's nice. You two can have a go at Chopsticks".

She laughed aloud and Ronald foolishly thought of several fantastic analogies that ranged far from the laugh itself. That dimple, like a facial umbilical scar that erased itself when the laugh stopped.

"What" he said loath to end the conversation, "do you do around here for pasttime?"

"Oh ... there isn't a lot to do. I like to walk in the woods, swim, watch the ants and squirrels and other wild things. I like to read." Her face fell a little, "but Dad doesn't like for me to read things I like. I've read classics until they come out of my ears".

"What do *you* like?"

She stretched her arms up in a delightful gesture that stretched the dress tightly across her young breasts. "I like adventurous things where men fight for women and make love to them ... Her face turned pink again and she sucked her breath in sharply. "Dad says that's wrong".

Ronald frowned. "Why?"

"I'm not sure. He says that evil comes from embrace." She closed her arms as though embracing some imaginary Casanova. "Do you think it's wrong?"

"I do not. In fact I write just such stories as you like".

She gasped. "Summerville ... Did you write "A Night in Peshawar?"

"Yes. I think it was my fourth or fifth. Did you like it?"

Her hands went slowly to her face that was now scarlet. "I loved it" she whispered. "I've read it a dozen times. It's all to pieces. I liked the way Hammond Elgin made love to the Indian girl ..."

She turned and raced away, her hair standing out in the breeze and her dress flying up exposing round delightful thighs that could stand a little more flesh. Ronald frowned, concentrating. Indian girl ... Hammond Elgin ... Then he remembered and turning almost ran himself. That had been probably the hottest love scene he had ever penned and the editors half reading the manuscript had missed it. When the book came out they nearly fainted but it was too late to stop it.

As he walked back down the path he could feel the stinging warmth of the sun penetrating his clothes but it failed to relax him. His hands insisted in balling up and the muscles between his shoulders began to ache. He shook himself and by pointed effort managed to relax a little. He kept seeing the dimple in her cheek, the flash of her even teeth, the limitless depths of her eyes framed in soft dark lashes. Tight again. He wiped his face for the third time then got up and ten minutes later he received another shock. The front door had accidently locked so he pressed the bell button totally unprepared for the person who answered the ring.

She was lighter than John and her skin had an arresting glow, a smoothness that seemed almost a sheen. Her eyes were black with abnormally long lashes and her face wore a placid serenity that seemed false because he could see the smouldering volcanos in the depths of her eyes.

She smiled slowly, "You are Mr. Ronald". Her voice was rich, musical and perfectly modulated.

"Yes. I guess I locked myself out".

"We rarely lock doors in this country" she said as he came into the living room. "Mr. Berry is at breakfast".

He walked into the kitchen and took a seat across from his brother, still in a faint daze from the impact of two beautiful women in the same hour. He glanced at the girl as she worked running a water mop over the tiles of the floor. She had a body that could only be described as extravagant. Lush full breasts that held her blue uniform out in twin peaks, fighting the tension provided by the belt that pulled the garment in sharply, at the slim waist, symmetrical hips softly rounded that flowed in pure curves into the contours of her thighs. The same pure lines descended into the calves of her legs. Her ankles were slim, like a dancer's and her small feet were encased in soft shapeless moccasins ... something like those Ferris had worn.

"Breakfast," said Berry quietly and Ronald was rudely jerked from his reverie. He glanced at his brother shamefacedly then began eating.

They sat on the north end of the porch and smoked silently for a while looking out across the vast expanse of the valley before them then Berry spoke. "From the close attention you were giving Mart in the kitchen it would appear that my fears were well founded".

Ronald sighed. "I was braced for that remark but I wasn't braced for Mart. She's rather· breathtaking, isn't she?"

"Rather," replied Berry shortly. "She did a fine job of taking my breath".

"Twice in one morning is plenty" mused Ronald lighting another cigarette.

"Twice … what do you mean?"

"I met a neighbor this morning. They live that way". He waved a hand toward the southeast. "An old bird who talks to God every morning about his lost Sally. He asked me if I'd seen her. I hadn't of course. She'd been dead thirty years. If that wasn't enough out pops this wood nymph who put wrinkles in my bones. Then I come in and get slapped in the face with Mart."

"About this other girl. What's she like?"

"A naiad, a sprite with gunmetal hair and eyes that are almost the same color. Skin like Jersey cream. She's a pastel fairy and she has a father who must be a character. Used to be a professor at some state university. He got in some trouble and either resigned or got fired. He has reared her under the tenet that men are bastards and the man-woman embrace is evil. She, however, is a little too healthy minded for any such guff as that to stick. She had read 'A Night in Peshawar', one of the hottest numbers I ever put out."

"What happened then?"

Ronald opened a hand and looked at the sweat glistening there. "She blushed and took off".

"Is she one of these non-virgin virgins you mentioned as we got off the train?"

"Berry, you can be singularly dense. This is no ordinary hayseed wench or product of a small town".

"How do you know? As I understand it you've seen her once".

Ronald made a despairing gesture. "Call it intuition if you wish. Call it anything. I *know*".

Berry thumped his cigarette into the yard. "Did you invite her over?"

"I did. She says she plays a little ... the piano I mean".

Berry grinned. "Then we have something in common and since you have decided that the hermit's existence is the thing for you ..."

Ronald got up and walked out into the brilliant sunshine. Walking on the crisp grass felt like treading the nap of a priceless rug. "Go to hell, brother" he said in a tight voice. "I'm going walking".

He walked aimlessly into the woods finally stifling the overpowering anger which Berry's joking remark had set afire.

He went further until a gigantic animal standing in the middle of the path stopped him. It was a Brahma bull of truly titanic proportions. Again Ronald felt the chill sweat of fear creep down his back, like ants marching toward another victory for his yellow streak, then the animal with a snort turned and walked off into the woods disdaining to attack this trembling creature whose smell was pungent with the acid tang of terror.

He came to the bottom of the hill and found a small narrow stream that rushed along with gurgles and murmurs, stopping to rest in still dark pools before continuing its complaining journey. He had paralleled the stream for a ways when he heard the sharp crack of a smallbore rifle. He stiffened and stood undecided for a moment then cursing the impulse to flee walked stiffly toward the sound.

He tried to laugh it off but the laugh cracked up and scattered making him feel silly ... and he was still afraid. He came to a large clearing dotted with patches of blackberry briars and wild azalea ... then he saw her. She had changed from the green cotton dress and now only wore faded shorts that had once been jeans and a sleeveless ragged chambry shirt. She placed the rifle against a tree and built a small fire with the sure touch of an expert and soon had a merry blaze going. She stopped and picked up her game, a cottontail rabbit and with deft movements stripped it of hide. She opened the abdomen and with a twitch of her wrist hurled the intestines into a bush. She took the carcass down a cow path to the water's edge and washed it with care and thoroughness.

She came back, hung the rabbit on a sharp twig and did things to the fire. As it settled down to a bed of coals she improvised a spit to which she attached the rabbit then after carefully salting and peppering it she placed it over the fire supported by two forked sticks. Slowly she turned it until it was a nice brown. From her pockets she brought a small package which contained several biscuits which she placed carefully on a log. By this time the rabbit was done to her liking so she removed it from the fire and swung it in the air for a while to cool it then started eating. He shuddered as she tore at the meat with her gleaming teeth, like a savage thing, wolfing great bites as though starved. Not until the last bone had been picked clean did she stop eating.

She stood up and glanced lazily about, a look of gluttonous satisfaction on her face, almost as though she had embraced a lover.

She walked out on a narrow beach and stood looking at the water and making childish faces at a small blue heron that sat perched on a dead snag, ignoring her. She sat down and slowly removed her shoes and until she had performed this act Ronald had not realized her intention. She was going to swim. He stiffened and felt a wave of shamed blood mount to his face. A peeping tom ... but he continued to watch a feeling of almost anesthetic detatchment coming over him. She slid the shorts down, followed them with the shirt and stood there in the sun, her body a slim graceful morsel of feminine witchery. Now that it was all revealed she seemed to lose some of the impression of undernourishment. She was an entity now complete without the distorting effect of clothes and the full impact of her classic sculpture struck him. She sat and toyed with her toes for a moment accomplishing the act with such utter grace that Ronald had to forcibly unclench his fists noticing that again they were dank with nervous sweat.

Finished with her play she leaped to her feet and dashed to the edge of the sand, rose like a bird, arched, and clove the water cleanly. She whirled and played about like a sportive duckling then came back to the sand where she stripped the water from her body with slender hands.

Then a third ingredient entered the tableau. A man walked from the brush to Ronald's left and crept up behind the unsuspecting girl. He was thick of shoulder and his legs suggested power. He wore khaki pants and shirt, cheap cowboy boots and on his head was a rancher's hat curled up on the sides. She saw him and with a gasp that was half a scream snatched up her clothes and backed away, covering herself as best she could.

"You look good, Ferris" he said ingratiatingly. "Don't run off no more. Me and you could have a big time together if you wasn't such a fraidy cat. What's wrong with a little lovin'?"

"Go away Bud," she said coolly. "My first experience with you was quite enough."

He stopped advancing and removed his hat his breath coming in short heated gasps. "Ferris, I aim to get you one way or 'nuther. Told you that before. I got to have you. I dreams about you and can't sleep half the time thinkin' about you the way you look when you swim and … Gosh, you're so purty." He licked his lips and a fresh resolve seemed to strike him. "Just once Ferris ... you don't know anything about it. You don't know what a man in love can do."

"I know what he won't do," she shot back. "Not to me at any rate. One of these days I'm going to kill you ..." She gasped, remembered, and ran like a deer for her rifle where it stood beside the gum tree. He must have divined her intention because he took after her and he could run. He was close on her when she reached the rifle. She came up with it just as he crashed into her. The barrel clipped him a solid blow over the left ear but flew from her hand with the impact as did her clothes. He managed to keep his feet and as she turned to run again he reached out and brought her into a bear-like embrace. She fought and clawed but he pinioned her arms subduing her eventually as she grew tired and fell limply to her knees.

He was panting and blood ran down the side of his face from four long furrows her sharp nails had left in his face. He nearly winded himself but he released her and stood over her like a victorious dog daring the loser to move. "Now" he said gutturally. "That ought to hold you for a while." He took off his shirt while she watched him in paralyzed fascination. He removed his pants and stood before her in shorts, the sun gleaming on his thick bulky muscles.

"Now baby," he cooed. "I been waitin' a long time for this. I don't even hold it against you for fightin'. That always makes it better."

It released the paralysis and she leaped to her feet but he was too quick for her. Again she fought hysterically, clawing and biting, her slim body contorted into stria of steely muscles as she battled against over-whelming odds. He laughed triumphantly and crushed her close to his chest ... the one mistake he made. With a sudden jerk and twist she drew her head down and seized one of his breasts and clamped down on it like a snapping turtle. Bud released her and swayed bawling like a branded steer, his arms high in the air like a particularly melodramatic wrestler registering phony agony only this agony was real. Had she been instructed by an expert she could not have found a tenderer place to assault and she gave it the best she had. Blood began to pour from around her mouth and his screams took on a hoarse despairing quality. She held on for another few seconds then with a spring like a deer she was gone and the woods swallowed her.

He fell to the ground on his knees and sobbed brokenly, leaning sideways to favor his terribly lacerated breast.

In his hiding place Ronald went slowly to his knees and fought to get the sweat from his eyes. His face was as pale as dough and his stomach reeled from the assault of a nausea that had many causes. He was weak, slaughtered, a vast flood of biting hate rising like vitriol in his throat. Staggering like a drunk man he turned and made his way back up the hill.

CHAPTER FIVE

It was nearly noon when he struggled up the final rise and stood panting on the brow of the hill. From there to the house would be level ground and for this he heaved a sigh of thanks. He was just about at the limit of his endurance which since his illness had been sorely reduced.

A truck stood back of the house near a brand new pen and in it long slender legged Tamworth hogs were strolling unconcernedly. Hogs ... He shuddered and made his way to the house where he was met and given entry by Mart, her soft black eyes deep with concern. "Is something the matter, sir?"

"Hell no," he snarled and felt the thick suffocating ache of pleasure stiffen his throat knowing that he had hurt her.

She stood silently back and let him in her face blank with the pain of his abrupt reply. Her head dropped a little as she walked back to the kitchen.

Ronald went to his bedroom and stood shaking, clinging to the bedpost until he could regain some semblance of control. For a while he fought his nerves and the knot which had started in his stomach while he watched the savage scene near the creek. Swiftly he turned and just made it to the bathroom where he vomited with such vigor that his ears rang and brilliant gold dots and geometric figures clouded his sight. He went to the bed and sprawled out on the cool white counterpane letting a trembling wrist wipe slime from his mouth. For a long time he lay as though in a coma then he got sick again. After the second effort which raised only a mouthful of bitter bubbles he stretched out on the tile floor and all went black for some time.

He came back to consciousness stimulated by the cold cloth that Berry was passing over his face.

"Decided to come out of it? Need a doctor?"

"You didn't go to hell like I said," Ronald said accusingly. "I do need a doctor, quarts of it. Dr. Barleycorn."

"You sound like a man I once knew who proved to be an ass of really heroic proportions."

"I know ... and his name was and is Ronald Summerville." Ronald got up. "Where do you keep the whiskey?"

"It's lunch time ..." Berry lifted his nostrils. "But I doubt that you'll be wanting any."

"I asked you about some whiskey."

"Okay son, if that's what you want. I'm going to eat. Johnny has chicken pie, hot rolls, snap beans and strawberry shortcake."

"I don't give a damn if he has barbecued maiden breast. I want whiskey."

"Whiskey it'll be. Go sit in the living room and think carefully about nothing for some time."

"That's a deal." He showered and still unsteady on his feet but somewhat relieved in the stomach he went out and chose a deep comfortable chair pushing it close to the glass front of the living room. He drew the curtains all around until it was half dark.

He sat in the chair, made an effort to relax and thought he had succeeded in part at least until he glanced at his hands. They were balled up again tightly, the knuckles white. He opened them slowly and breathed several deep breaths. It always seemed to help, deep breathing, so he continued until his head began to swim then stopped and rested his head on the back of the chair. Ten minutes later Mart opened a card table and placed on it a pint of whiskey, a pitcher of water and a bowl of ice.

"Will that be all sir?"

Ronald twisted his hands together in torture. Her voice had been soft, compassionate with a depth of understanding that he could only guess.

He looked at her and saw the African inscrutability cover her nearly white face, like a cloud drawn over the moon. "Mart ... I'm sorry I barked at you."

"Yes sir."

He nodded. "All right, you're sore at me. I deserve it. Now go away and leave me alone."

"On the contrary, I'll do no such thing."

He blinked at the crisp crack of her rejoinder. He felt as though she had slapped him smartly.

"I don't get it."

"I said I'd do no such thing. You came in beaten to your knees for some reason. I'd like to know what it was."

"It has nothing to do with you."

"I'm sure of that but it has something to do with you. You're one of my employers and as such I have an interest ... or are you one of those strong silent men who are neither strong nor silent but cut all to pieces inside because you can't face up to the facts, because you can't admit to anything less than what your ego demands that you be."

This was no slap, rather a full armed blow. "Look here," he said sitting erect, angered. "I'll have you know ..." He sank back. "You're a good kid, Mart. Run along and leave me to my grief."

"That's not what I call it," she said as she turned away. Instantly she came back. "When you feel like talking about it I'm willing to listen ... Promise? It always takes a little fortitude to talk ... if you tell the truth and unless you tell the truth I'll know it immediately."

Quite without intending to he laughed. He did not feel like laughing but this was something he had never been prepared for.

"Promise, Mart. On my word."

"Good." She walked off leaving him to stare at the opacity of the heavy blue curtain.

Mart was a new deal in servants. The second time she had seen him and she ordered him around about his personal business. John had said she was hard-headed. He poured a strong highball, drank it too fast then poured another. The fire subsided presently settled to a smooth relaxing burn. Berry came in and sat beside him.

"Why all the gloom?" he asked.

"I like it that way."

"What's the drinking for?"

"I like it that way."

"What was the trouble this noon, sick, passing out on the bathroom floor?"

Ronald grunted and closed his eyes.

"Want to be alone," asked Berry.

"Yes."

"Fine. In that case I'll stay a while. Incidently you looked like a corpse when you came in."

"I'm not as good as a corpse. A corpse has certain soil enrichening properties. I don't even have that."

"As a corpse you do."

"As yet I'm not a corpse."

"What happened this morning to make you look like that and get sick?"

"Ferris."

"I thought she happened earlier."

"She did. Then she happened again. Something's screwy about … I don't know what but I watched her skin a rabbit, cook and eat it with great gulps as though she was starved. She does look a little on the skinny side … not that what she has isn't enough but there could be more."

"That doesn't seem like anything to get sick about. She didn't eat it raw, did she?"

"I told you, she cooked it. Then she went swimming …" He passed a shaky damp hand over his face. "… and I watched."

"Oh … you perfect *cad*," said Berry in a jibing falsetto.

"Cad? I wish that was all."

"Don't tell me you went in with her."

"No, some bruiser came up and caught her … still naked. Big muscular bastard. Held her until she was practically out on her feet then let her fall, stood over her like a victorious gladiator and took off his clothes."

"What were you doing all that time?" Berry was sitting on the edge of his chair, his nostrils compressed and white.

Ronald laughed hollowly and took a swig from his highball. "Me …? Why, I just cowered there in the brush and watched. What'd you expect a yellow crum like me to do, sally forth and save her virtue? I crouched there, felt my guts turn to water, then I started hating myself. I did such a good job that I made myself ill. Now … satisfied?"

Berry massaged the back of his neck, his big body taut. He had had a daughter who died a year before her mother. The girl would be about grown now. "So he raped her."

"No, but no thanks to me. He picked her up and was on the verge of it when she bit him right squarely over the left nipple. He bellowed like the Bull of Bashan but she held on until blood was running out of her mouth in a stream. When she turned him loose he wasn't even in shape to chase her."

"Who is he?"

"I'm not well acquainted with the local clench artists. I'll find out if it'll make you happy."

"What was he doing on my land?"

"How would I know? Maybe he thought it was his."

Suddenly Mart stood before them her breasts lifting to some inner tumult. "What'd he look like?"

"Red," said Ronald. "Beefy red with sand hair and firey gold hair on his arms. Dressed in some sort of cowboy rig, boots and hat."

"One of the Kitchens," she said through set teeth. "Sounds like Bud Kitchen. The same bunch that are always trying to get to me. Bud sets his mind on girls and gets them sometimes. He's like a hound dog on a trail. They're bad people."

Berry had grown paler, his big hands clenched in his lap. "Looks like we're going to have a grand time in these parts. Tell us something about these brigands, Mart."

Her lip curled. "Trash! Grandma calls them *buckras*. Poor white trash that make a lot of money stealing other people's cattle and making and selling whiskey. They're always after some girl ... white or black. Their older brother was killed when Mr. Earnest Johnson caught him on his front porch with his sixteen year old daughter. He had his hand over her mouth and was right ready to ..." Her eyes flashed and her lips tightened. "Mr. Johnson shot him."

Berry sat back in the chair and let his breath seep out. "That was stupid ... right on the front porch?"

"Well, Mr. Johnson had gone down in the field and there wasn't anybody else home. He just came back too soon." She turned and disappeared as suddenly as she had come.

"Yellow," said Ronald with finality. "I thought so for a long time. Now I know it. Standing there, not doing a thing. I'm not exactly a runt: I'm not a weakling."

"Maybe if he'd actually done it you would have done something."

"Me?" Ronald laughed bitterly. "How you talk." He made another drink and had taken the first sip when John came into the room. "There's a man out back to see you, Mr. Berry."

"Who is he?"

"I think he's a tenant over on the adjoining plantation. I've seen him in Tide."

Berry got up and went out the back onto another porch almost a duplicate of the one in front. A man stood in the shade of a crepe myrtle holding a battered brown hat in his hands. He was tall and thin with wispy grey hair and sharp nose. His eyes were bright and ferret-like but the rest of his face seemed to register stupidity.

"Mr. Summerville?"

"Yes. What can I do for you?"

The man fidgited and dragged a bare big toe through the grass. "I'm Bill Marks. I works on the halves fer Mrs. Potter. Thought mebbe you might need some day labor some time. I got some boys what's good hands … willin' workers. Got a coupla gals what does right nice house work, too."

Berry nodded for no particular reason. "Sorry Bill, I don't have any day work right now and I've got my house staffed already but … By the way, can your boys ride?"

"Well, sho they can. Been ridin' since they were kids."

"I'm supposed to have three hundred and eighty head of cattle and so far I haven't seen them."

"You want 'em driv up?"

"Not necessarily, but I would like to have a couple of boys ride out with me some day soon so we can get a partial count anyway. They have horses?"

"Plenty of hosses over at the place. Mrs. Potter'll lend 'em bosses."

"I need to buy a couple of horses too. Where's the best place around here to buy them?"

"Mr. Julie Root. He got a lot o' hosses ... cheap." Berry scratched his head. "I'm afraid I don't know a lot about buying horses ..."

"I'll go 'long with you," said Bill eagerly, leaning forward, his lanky body seeming to defy gravity. "I knows hosses."

"That'll be fine ..." Berry grinned. "Now I need a car."

"You can have mine," said John.

"I'll let you take me into Tide, Johnny, and I'll buy one. Bill will you be busy tomorrow morning?"

"No sir. I'll be right here ... When?"

"After breakfast, eight or nine. Guess I'd better get a trailer too."

"Sure will need one," averred Bill. "You'll need it to haul calves and such."

Ronald stepped out on the porch and squinted his eyes against the glare of the afternoon sun.

"Evenin' sir," said Bill bobbing his head. "Been talkin' to you' brother ... you's the other Mr. Summerville, ain't you?"

Ronald nodded and examined Bill without apparent care but he would remember exactly what he saw any time in the future if he needed it.

"Been tellin' him about my fine boys and gals. Boys can do most anything and the gals is good housekeepers. Purty fine lookin' gals too if I do say it myself." He snickered and rolled his eyes. "Mighty handy to have around the house."

"Come over in the morning," said Berry frowning at this obvious effort to play up the girls, "and we'll go pick out a couple of horses."

Bill nodded vigorously and slouched away taking in the pigs that lolled in the shade of a china tree inside their pen.

"Better watch those hogs," said Ronald, his mouth twisting with distaste. "He'll have them in a sack before you know it. Maybe the gals would come over and feed them if they could be assured of a little fun."

"I'll leave that department to you," said Berry shortly. "Feel better?"

"I'm drunk if that answers your question."

"It doesn't but let it ride. If you're through, Johnny, we'll duck over to Tide and see what we can find in the way of transportation. Want to go, Ron?"

"No. I'm going to stay and get drunker if possible." But he didn't. An hour later he was saying, "No ... I haven't seen Sally but I'll keep a sharp lookout."

Unker Ben nodded, shuffled away toward the bluff and out of the house came a man whom Ronald disliked immediately.

"Good evening" he said politely. "I'm Ronald Summerville ... a neighbor of one day."

"I have no neighbors," said the man harshly.

"Maybe you have no friends," snapped Ronald still too tight to be tolerant, "but you damn well have neighbors. Purely a matter of geographical juxtaposition."

The man came out on the veranda, his black close set eyes burning, his stiff black hair standing up like the ruff of a boar. "I might remind you that you're on my property ..."

"On the contrary, I'm on Unker Ben's property."

"I'm his legal heir and brother." The voice rose and trembled.

"So what? I guess you're Ferris' father and your name is Macklin."

"It is, not that it is any of your business and I'd better not catch you smelling in behind her inciting her to any evil doings."

Ronald laughed. "I think Ferris bathes regularly although I doubt that you do. I can smell you from here."

She came around the corner of the house and stopped short. Her face was still spotted with bruises and she was pale but otherwise she seemed unperturbed. "Dad ... why are you speaking so loud ... this is Mr. Summerville ..."

"I know who he is. I've told him to get off the property and not come back. I forbid you to speak to him."

She went paler still and caught her breath. She was afraid of him but her eyes apologized to Ronald ... begged him to leave and he could think of a number of good reasons why he should do so. He looked at her directly. "I feel sorry for you kid and ..." He let it hang hoping she would take it that he would help any way he could.

She nodded. "Please go now."

"Wait a minnit." Unker Ben had come up behind them. His eyes were not as vacant as they had been. "What you runnin' the man off for?"

"Because I ordered her to do it" said the brother. "I ordered her never to speak to this ... this ... whoever he is."

"Well, you must be a fool." Unker Ben frowned hazily. "The man's done promised to look out for Sally. You ain't forgot whose place this is, is you?"

The thin pinched face on the veranda grew hard. "I'm telling you, Ben, I won't have Ferris having anything to do with these nobodies. I've laid the law down."

Unker Ben walked closer to the steps and spat accurately, the tobacco juice exploding like a small watery bomb on the immaculate toes of Macklin's much polished shoes. "Shet up, Dowd. This here is my place. I pays the taxes and buys the vittles. All you could do was get a education and teach school. Then you had t' go get in trouble with some fool stunt with some young gal and they run you off."

Macklin swayed and his face turned purple. With a malevolent snort he turned and went back into the house.

Unker Ben had proven that although he might be a little touched on the subject of Sally he was still the man of the place. He grinned toothlessly at Ronald. "Keep on lookin', son. Both of us lookin' ... we might find her. 'Tain't no harm speaking to the gel. Right fetchin' gel she is too."

"I'd like to speak to her for a moment if I may," Ronald said tightly.

"Go ahead. Don't pay no mind to that there run off professer. Never was much t' im."

Out of sight of the house hidden by a dense sweet olive thicket he said. "I saw you eat the rabbit."

She went pale. "I ... you didn't speak ..."

"I was afraid I might frighten you. Ferris, what goes on here?"

Her shoulders slumped. "He's a vegetarian and won't let me eat meat."

"Why doesn't Unker Ben let you eat it? He seems to be the boss."

She shook her head. "He has sudden flashes like that but most of the time he just wanders around looking lost and asking God and everybody about Sally. If I didn't make him eat I believe he'd starve to death."

"All right. Come to the house when you can. Mrs. Hornsby stocked our freezer. You can have a steak and french fries any time you come. Make it every day if you wish."

Her eyes softened and glistened with moisture. "That is very kind of you ..."

"Berry ... that's my brother, call me Ron."

She smiled. "All right, Ron. Whenever, I get hungry I'll come over. Remember you told me to."

"I mean it, too. The thought of you being hungry for meat makes me ill."

"I think you're a little tight." Her smile apologized for the remark.

"I am." He cut if off because he did not want to discuss the reason for his drinking. "Can you get away when you wish?"

"Mostly. I have to be here at meal times to fix their food … such as it is. All Dad has done since we came here is to plant his garden and raise peanuts. There are plenty of pecans in season."

He studied her lips and could see the marks of tension around the corners. "We'll be looking for you, Ferris."

"I'll come. I promise."

He left walked through the path to the bluff and stood for a long time watching the shadows lengthen in the valley until they leapfrogged whole acres, then half a mile, then all that was left of the sun was gilded streaks that brushed long fingers over the green canvas.

Ronald sat on a blackened stump and shuddered so hard he felt as though a chill was coming on. Then quite unexpectedly he began to weep. He began to get frightened and got to his feet hoping to make it to the house so that at least he might die tidily and not have half the county searching for him. He almost ran along the path, his mind more and more confused until at last he seemed to run into *her.*

"Now, now" she said soothingly, holding him tightly to her breast. She was a firmament in chaos, a peak standing fast above the tumultuous waves that beat him from the inside. When full clear consciousness finally permeated the numbness of his being he was stretched on his bed … undressed. He lay quietly and listened to the first lashing whip of the wills-a-widow that came sweetly, clearly through the window across the open meadow, freighted in on a cool twilight breeze. Bit by bit he began to reconstruct things from the moment she had held him close ... to the strengthening softness of her motherly caresses that gradually grew less motherly until the satin of her breasts created a back fire that was gradually fed by greater portions of her becoming available to his mad eagerness, then the whole glory of her creamy voluptuousness, the power and eagerness of the woodland love which she provided and the smashing release of damned up passion, the anesthetic release to his nerves. Now he felt that he had none.

She appeared at the doorway and strangely he did not leap over and cover himself. Peace was too great and he was too weary of strife.

"Supper is ready," she said softly. She did not turn and leave hurriedly because of his nakedness, but stood and waited for his answer. He sat up slowly. "You're rather a wonderful person. Thanks. I think I was a candidate for a padded cell when you found me. And the cure ... How did you know?"

"I know those things. I don't know how. I can sense when a man needs me."

"Don't you ever need a man?"

Her smile was misty. "Always. Not just any man though. I'm a very particular woman."

"Thank God for you," he said profoundly.

"I'll be around." She came to him and stroked his forehead and allowed him to pull her close to feel the warmth of her again and sense the rich fullness of her body. "Supper's ready," she repeated, "and you should eat, especially after that drinking."

"I'll be there in a shake."

He dressed and went to the kitchen where Berry was already seated. "Well … you look like a rescued mariner. What happened?"

"Something very wonderful," said Roanld profoundly. "Something that is a secret and let's let it go at that."

"By all means. I got a car today."

"Good. You might need one."

"You can use it."

"What would I use it for?"

"You might take Ferris to a show or something."

"Not a chance. I met Macklin today and he's a screwball of the best blood. He's a vegetarian and won't let her eat meat so she steals out and kills game and eats it. She's coming here for a square meal …"

"I already am here," she said with a laugh as she came through the door. "Am I in time?"

They stood up. "Ferris," said Ronald. "This is my brother Berry, John our cook and Mart, who does everything."

Ferris smiled exhibiting the dimple and said. "How do you do," to everyone with impartiality then she looked at the table with its huge beef roast, mashed potatoes, tossed salad, hot rolls and iced tea.

She was dressed in a simple little frock of cool green and white print with an off the shoulder neck that revealed the marble smooth skin of her throat and shoulders. She sat in the chair Ronald held for her and smiled shyly across the table at Berry. "I hope you don't mind."

"The only time I'll mind is when you're not here," he said gallantly. "You lend something to the table."

"What will your father say?" asked Ronald taking his seat.

"He won't know. Luckily I'm such a rambler both day and night that he doesn't think anything of it when I leave the house.

As long as he's fed, can have his garden and write monographs on cultish nonsense which no one buys then he's not cast down. I doubt that he was ever happy."

She ate. Ronald remembering it later could not recall that he had ever seen a slender switch of a girl eat like a G. I. on leave from Army chow. Three big slabs of roast beef, a little potatoes and one roll. "It's the meat I crave," she had said, "Other things take up room."

She had eaten two huge saucers of cherry ice cream, too, apologizing for her appetite.

Later they sat on the porch and listened to the night hawks whispering "spew" then watched them fall into headlong dives with most unbirdish bellows at the bottom then the graceful climb back to the heights to repeat the operation. Silence lasted some time then Berry got up. "I'm bushed," he apologized. "I think I'll turn in."

"Oh ... is it bed time."

"For him only," said Ronald quickly. "I never go to bed this early."

"Good night Ferris, be sure to come again."

"Thank you so much, Mr. Summerville," she said softly. "I will come again and you must play for me."

Berry turned pink. "I'm just a doodler, I don't really play."

"So he says," put in Ronald. "He's good."

Berry made a disparaging noise and went into the living room.

"I think nights are always lovely," she said settling back in the bamboo chair. "Even when it storms and the lightning lashes all over and thunder rolls. Even when it rains torrents and its cold, even when snow falls and hisses ... you think it hisses because it seems that it should."

"Right! They are always beautiful and maybe it is because what we can't see we imagine and imaginings are beautiful. Daylight robs the imagination and paints pictures without compromise because they are too clear. At night we need only a suggestion then we make it whole with imagination."

"You have beautiful thoughts, Ron."

"Thank you. Your own beautiful thoughts accelerated mine. You not only have beautiful thoughts but you are a beautiful woman."

He could see her fingers tighten on the arm of the chair. "No one ever told me that before."

"But you know it."

"Let's say I hoped it."

"And why did you hope it?"

A shy smile moved her lips. "Maybe because I read a book of yours and read what a wonderful thing a beautiful woman means to a man. Maybe men are necessary to me and I must be beautiful to attract them. Maybe because I know the frosting is the first thing one notices about a cake."

He tightened, he himself had used that phrase before. "How does it feel to know one is beautiful?"

"It feels good. It gives me a sense of belonging, of being something not seen everyday. It makes me think thoughts that Dad would beat me for if he knew. It makes me realize that I am a woman and a woman is both necessary and desirable ... and yet I haven't the faintest notion how to flirt."

"Lack of practice," he said with a chuckle that sounded a little loose and crazy. Talking to Ferris was something that he could not quite take with his old ease. From her own beauty of body and mind to the bluntness of her frank speech she was an enigma because of the total lack of enigmatic impression. Some people were so fundamental that the very lack of mystery and complexity disarmed people with whom they were associated thus they were more enigmatic than a more complex personality. "You started reading the wrong things."

"No. I started reading the right things. Do you have any more of your books."

"Yes."

"May I read them?"

"Of course but I hope they don't put ideas in your head. You see a woman's mind is a peculiar thing. It picks up impressions and with an emotional push makes them seem too important. For instance I knew a girl once, a perfectly healthy lovely girl who was raped. To this day sex is something frightening and terrible. She was ruined." He glanced at her out of the corner of his eye.

She sat as taut as a bowstring and her knuckles went white. "It could do that I suppose, to some. I think in my mind, though, rape would be severely kept as such. I think I could divorce it from the real thing. You see, several attempts have been made on me. There is no one around to protect me in that way. Uncle Ben is too old and Dad would turn purple and blame me for it."

Ronald felt the first trickle of sweat start down his back and he forced his fingers loose from the arms of the chair. "What a hell of a dirty shame. What a beastly rotten thing … what a state of mind to live with … Does it threaten all the time?"

"Oh no, but I like to wander and I've been caught off from home. I like to swim naked and I've been caught in the creek. I can't quit and some day he will catch me. I know it."

For a moment he felt like his supper would come up but the nausea passed as she continued to talk but he heard little of what she said.

"I don't know what sort of man I'll marry," she said soberly. "I don't even know if I will marry." She leaned forward, her face close to his. "Ron, don't you believe that if I don't a perfectly good woman will have gone to waste?"

"There can be little doubt."

"Now I think I'll go home," she said standing and smoothing the dress down her long straight thighs.

"I'll go along ..." He almost said, "for protection" but the abject cowardice of that afternoon came back and choked the words down his throat.

"You don't have to." She wanted him to badly but it seemed an imposition. She often rambled at night and was never afraid. Not even of Bud Kitchen because at night she felt quite safe, under the blanket of darkness.

"Of course I don't have to, I happen to want to."

They walked down the dim path, dim because the only illumination was from the brilliant candelabra of stars overhead. Their hands touched, leaped apart then touched again. After several times they finally clung, stiffly at first like the nose meeting of a pair of strange dogs then they relaxed and Ronald felt as though his left hand had been seared.

Her fingers twined with his after the first shyness was overcome and they walked closer together because of the linkage. At one point along the path the bluff cut sharply inward and he shrank away from it as though it was endowed with some force that might drag him over the brink.

She stopped and faced him. "Ron, tell me what's the matter."

"Why ... what do you mean?"

"I followed you yesterday and watched you sit right here and cry. I know something's wrong ... very wrong." Her face was close to his. "Can't I do something to help? Isn't there something I can say or do or ..." Her face was young but so serious, youthful and tender but still mature and womanly. Woman, the healer, the dryer of tears, the haven from the snarling biting snapping world of competition. Ronald felt weak and giddy, touched to his depths and particularly loaded with a sense of unworthiness.

Her hands went to his shoulders and her face came even closer. "Why don't you tell me about it."

He sighed. "Let's sit here." A great log lay almost across the path and they sat, still very close.

"It's a long story." He said helplessly.

"I'm in no hurry."

"Could you love a coward?"

"That would depend on a lot of things. What sort of coward?"

"In the warp and the woof, toe to scalp. The big hero with a chest full of medals turns into a guy who runs from a firecracker. Who jumps when a door slams." He drew in a deep breath and leaped.

He told her everything, in all the sordid details, the defalcations of Madelyn, his own weaknesses, and finally why they had come to Mississippi.

"When we get here I find that I'm no better. I actually …" No, he couldn't tell her that his cowardice extended to letting Kitchen have his way with her while he stood sweating in the brush, watching.

"What?"

"Nothing. Just another depth I'd as soon not go into."

"Ron, I'm not an educated person. I can speak well, and I read but something tells me that you didn't tell all. You're too cruel and hard on yourself. You haven't gone far enough into the details of why you're that way. There must be some answer, some turning point, some little thing that will show you differently. I can't believe that a man who writes beautifully about strong men and lovely women who love strong men could be essentially a weakling."

"Maybe I wrote about it so much because I subconsciously realized I was a coward and tried to compensate."

She shook her head. "My opinion of a coward is a person who would move heaven and earth to keep it from showing. Who would so overdo bravado that anyone would know something was wrong."

"I did. That's why I was such a fool during World War II. Trying to show off, being very lucky, the right officer in attendance. I guess you put your finger on it all right. In Korea it was there for everyone to see and I can't deny it."

"It doesn't fit what I feel," she said, "and I know I'm right. Let's go."

They walked on in silence still holding hands like adolescents, thrilling much after the fashion of the very young stealing forbidden goodies.

At the clearing in front of the Macklin house she turned and looked up into his eyes. "Thank you."

His eyes opened wider. "What for?"

"For the supper, that wonderful meat, for talking to me like I was a person and not an idiot, for telling me I'm beautiful, for telling me what's in your heart. Thank you, thank you, thank you."

She reached up and kissed him softly on the lips and stood back, her eyes as starry as any orb above them. "Thank you again, Ron ..."

"Look." He cried desperately, "do you know what you're doing to me?"

Her lips parted and a look of immense gratitude flooded her face. "Oh Ron ... am I doing something?"

"You have no idea." He caught her and crushed her close but he didn't kiss her. He let his lips wander in caresses over her forehead, into the depths of her fragrant hair, finally, as she tilted her head, her lips parted and her eyes closed, to her mouth where he lurched to the terrific thrust of emotion that flamed inside him like a torch. Her lips were soft, amateurish and quiescent. But no lips he had ever touched drove him so near the brink of madness.

Gently she forced him away and stood back, her breath coming in labored gasps. "Oh Ron ... do you know what I want?"

He swallowed, feeling that he had let things go too far, unwilling to answer her question. She reached back, released a snap and opened the front of her dress, gave him a momentary glimpse of her young breasts hardened by passion, then she turned and fled into the night.

He passed a trembling hand over his face and sat abruptly in the dew drenched grass. For a long time he sat, coming by degrees back to normal then feeling that he could safely do so he stood up and walked slowly back to the path.

CHAPTER SIX

He wondered what she'd think of him had he told her of his supreme moment of cowardice. The possibilities shocked him and he resolved never to tell her.

He walked a while and feeling tired, rested, leaning against the smooth hole of a flowering dogwood, and tried to identify this feeling he had for Ferris. It was not the same thing he had felt for Madelyn, of that he was certain.

Suddenly the skin of his body contracted and a damp sheen stood out on his face. There was someone or something very close, so close he felt he could feel its breath, and hear it. With clock-like slowness he turned. It was there sure enough, and two widespaced eyes had caught the reflection from the stars and burned intensely like green lamps. For a moment he stood rigid and cold paralyzed with fear, then the beast gave a snort and shook its great head. With a despairing bleat Ronald broke and ran as he had never ran before in his life. The path curved to the left to escape the encroaching hemisphere of erosion where it bit out an area of the bluff but Ronald could not turn and for the second time in two nights he went headlong into the blackness of the void.

He struck a sharp angle of eroded clay, bounded off turned over completely and landed with a dry crash in a dense bed of blackberry vines.

When he recovered consciousness he attempted to move and a thousand thorns denied him the pleasure. For the better part of half an hour he struggled gingerly with the briars, wincing and sweating from the pain in his chest. It cut his breath short and deep breathing was out of the question. Finally he made it then remembering his previous climb and the encounter with a near-snake, looked at the towering wall above him and shook his head. Somewhere through the woods to his right was a road and that if followed long enough would bring him to Little River Plantation. He reeled against a tree and fell to his knees, slid further and found that the leaves were soft and inviting. In a few minutes he had fallen into a deep sleep.

At dawn he awoke, stiff, so sore that he almost cried out when he tried to get up, feverish and pervaded by a crushing malaise that hung heavy over him like a wet blanket.

He managed to locate the road off to his right and toward this he made his way. After half a mile of hard walking, painful breathless walking, a rattletrap of a car pulled alongside him and stopped. "Jeepers, Mr. Ronald, what are you doing out here this time of day?"

It was John and the open door looked inviting. Ronald almost fell into the car and leaned back a feeling of intense relief flooding his aching body. "Went over the thrice damned cliff again," he said. "Bull … I think, scared me half to death and I ran … right off into thin air. This time I bounced around on the ground for a while before doing a flip into a briar patch. I've got exactly half a million of them in my skin at the moment. Where've you been?"

"I spent the night at Mamma's."

"Mart not with you?"

"No sir. She didn't go … you sure you're all right?"

"If there's anything I'm dead certain of at the moment it is, indisputably, that I am not all right. I'm dead. It hasn't occurred to me to stop breathing yet."

John, not knowing what reply to make to that rather peculiar statement kept silent and they went on up the hill and turned left through the cattle gap.

Bill Marks was already there, his elbows hooked over the wire of the pig pen watching the long red animals with interest.

Mart came out of the kitchen and looked at Ronald with troubled eyes. "Mr. Berry's gone to look for you, Mr. Ronald. He's worried to death."

"Sorry and all that," he said tightly. "I didn't run off the bluff on purpose." He walked ten feet toward her and fell forward on the grass, unconscious.

"Shock, exposure and three broken ribs," said the tired faced young man dressed in a baggy linen suit. "With rest he'll be all right in a few days but he'll breathe softly for a while."

The room was small and white and neat, smelling, of course, like all hospital rooms. Ronald felt as though he was in a plaster cast, weak, groggy and aching with shame.

The doctor went out and Ronald looked across the room where Berry sat looking at a newspaper. "How did I get here," he askesd with peculiar breathlessness due to his taped ribs.

"Johnny and I brought you. You messed up my horse buying spree and Bill Marks was no end put out."

"He'll live," said Ronald shortly. "As soon as I can get the hell up from here I'm leaving."

"Where will you go?"

"Some place where I can wander around and not fall off bluffs, where bulls don't stalk me and snort me out of my senses, where I can get some peace."

Berry nodded. "Go ahead," he said with great calm. "Me, I'm staying here. I'm tickled as a kid with a new tricycle with the idea of rising early and being a gentlemen rancher. By the way, the mayor came to see you."

"So what …? I can't vote for him. Why'd he come?"

"Just being neighborly. He'd heard of us through the Hornbys. Remember, he was the only calm man in town the day of the twister."

"I remember. I don't want people ducking in and out of here all the time. How long will I have to stay?"

"You could go now but the ride'd shake you up and grit the ends of those ribs together."

Ronald closed his eyes. "You needn't be so graphic. I'll stay quietly. Why don't you beat it and get your horses? I'll be all right."

"Anything you want?"

"Nothing but quiet and solitude. When you leave I'll have that."

Berry left but Ronald discovered that he was wrong. A student nurse kept popping in and out asking him how he felt, if he wanted icewater, a Coke or anything. She was cute with a saucy little nose, gleaming blonde hair and clear faultless skin. Her legs were good stout pins with trim ankles and her uniform was obliged to fit her curves. Her's was one of those bodies that everything fits one way or another. Her uniform, he was afraid, might burst at certain strategic points like high in front and half way down behind.

"And how do we feel since the tape is on?"

"I'm not a crystal gazer," he muttered crossly, "so I don't know how you feel. I feel like hell."

"Oh come," she said putting her hands on her smoothly rounded hips. "You should have seen the man who came in yesterday, bones all sticking through his skin and I don't know what all. A log rolled on him."

"Why don't you roll him in and shock me back to uncon-sciousness," he snapped. "Are you always this attentive to your patients?"

"The cute ones ... always."

Ronald blushed and the girl laughed delightedly. "He's shy," she bubbled and swept out her starched uniform rustling cleanly.

He cursed under his breath, changed positions gingerly then changed back and sighed. Three or four days to lay in this white room badgered ceaselessly by nurses who liked to be attentive to cute patients. Cute! He snorted and winced as a pain stabbed him.

"Hurt much?"

He looked toward the door and saw a round beaming face full of good nature and inquisitiveness. In the face reposed a dead cigar which made him think of the Mayor.

"Sometimes. Let the rest of you dribble on in so I won't get the twisted idea that you're nothing but a face."

The body was as round and good natured as the face. "I'm Charley Olsen, Mr. Summerville. Mayor of Tide." He thrust out a soft fat hand which Ronald was morally certain would be flabby. It was anything but flabby and he took a new inter-est in Charley Olsen. "Hear tell you're the feller who writes them books you can find in any drugstore. Been a fan of yours for a long time. 'Specially them foreign stories ... India, Africa ... Places like that always had a hook into me. Far as I ever been is Birmingham and New Orleans. Drop down to New Orleans ever' now and then to ... Heh, heh ... sorta play around a little. Gets a man outa the rut."

"Thanks," said Ronald. "Do you make it a habit to visit every-one who comes here?"

"Nunno. Once in a while I come around and sorta glad-hand folks. Don't hurt me none and they do get kinda lonesome."

"We arrived in a dead heat with the twister. I guess you still have some here from that blow."

"Two or three," he said rolling the cigar. "Tore up a bunch of shanties. Old Mrs. Nelson … been living at the Hotel for years, got scared when that telephone pole went through the window. Tried to climb out and got tangled in the wires. Lightning struck and killed her."

"Yes, I saw it. I also noticed that you seemed to be the only one not completely mad."

Charley made a depreciatory face. "People's like that. Don't know what happened to me but once I'd of been the scaredest one of the bunch."

Ronald grew attentive. "What do you mean?"

Charley chuckled and wheezed a little. "Oh … they calls it battle fatigue now but in Warld War I it was shell shock. Made up my own mind that shell shock was a bad term 'cause … well I was bounced around some with H. E. but who the hell wasn't in the Argonne? Reckon it's a matter of maturity or glands, or your outlook or something. One day I was scared of my shadow and the next I had to pistol whip Alex Kitchen and I done it. I was marshal then. Ain't been bothered since. I sorta made me a formula to go by. Getting scared can injure you worse'n what you're scared of. Like old Mrs. Nelson … Like Gus Starke trying to climb to her rescue with her dead as a salted mackerel and what does he do but grab a hot wire."

"I was in the station, looking. Saw it all."

"Well, there you are. Just like I said, fear hurts more people than what they are feared of."

Ronald's eyes narrowed. "You talked to my brother, didn't you?"

Charley nodded. "Wasn't much of a talk. I asked him how you was doing and stuff like that."

"He didn't tell you how I got hurt?"

"No. Don't believe we got that far along. Dr. Castle come in about then and they started talking. How did you get hurt?"

Ronald grimaced. "Just like you said. A bull snorted at me in the night and I ran off the cliff ... bluff. Whatever you want to call it. Scared the lights out of me."

The Mayor nodded. "It'll happen ever' time."

"Do you know why I'm here, I mean out at Little River?"

"Nope. Your brother, neither. Y'all came from Ohio, I think, and you brought money with you. You gave a lot of men work building your house and you both seem like respectable citizens. That's enough for me."

"Thanks, Charley. Just the same since you seem to know something about the anatomy of fear I'll tell you a story."

When the story ended Charley nodded. "Not too different from me.... but, son, you going to find it kinda hard to live with yourself for a while on account of that business of letting Bud Kitchen mix it up with that pore little Macklin girl without giving her a hand.

"Heard y'all hired Johnny Patterson and his sister."

"That's right. Johnny's a top notch cook."

"Good boy. Whole family is as fine a bunch of Negroes as you'll find in the county. Respectable, hard workers, and they try to see that the kids get a education."

"They seem to be nearer white than black."

"They is. Old man Howard Patterson was a farmer and raised Devon cows. A white man, police juror, school board and all. Left a lot of money but none to the second family. Martha ... that's the kids Ma was as fine looking a mulatto as you ever seen in your life and the kids took after her. That girl you got working for you'll take any white girl in the county for looks. I brung up the subject to sorta hand out a little warning. Them Pattersons ain't the sort to drift around with just any dawg that squats in their front yard and Mart has had a hard time dodging white men. Them Kitchens been after her and they ain't going to stop just 'cause she's working for y'all."

"They'd better," said Ronald with more heat than he intended, making Charly raise an eyebrow. "What I mean is," he continued somewhat flustered, "Berry's an easy going sort but something like that would make him go on the prod. They'd better forget about her."

"They ain't and I'd bet on it. Somebody'll have to kill off a couple more of 'em before they learns any sense." Charley got up. "Guess I'll be going. Don't want to tire the patient. Anything I can do for you?"

"No. I'll just lay around here a few days and then go home when I'm in shape."

"Grub ain't too hot in this place. I know. I was here when I had my appendix out. Reckon I'll drop by tonight with a little lunch for you. My wife is a mighty good cook."

"I'd hate to put her or you to any trouble."

He shrugged. "She wanted me to bring it in time for dinner but I told her you probably wasn't too hungry right after you got hurt. Mr. Summerville, if there is anything I can do for you boys just say the word. I know you're new down here and might feel a little stiff about asking favors but if I can give a hand at any time I'll be proud to do it."

"That's swell of you Charley … and my name is Ronald. Berry calls me Ron. If there's anything we need we'll call on you. You might tell me what we can expect from the Kitchens."

"Well … take Solomon to do that, but there'll be trouble.

The nurse popped back in. "Had a nice visitor?"

"Very nice and because you people serve patients gunk he's going to bring me my supper."

"Pity the poor nurses," she said with a grimace. "They have to eat it unless some kind soul takes them out to eat."

"Don't your cute patients take you out?"

"Occasionally, then they want my fair body in exchange for the meal ... usually."

"And you don't trade in any such unfair terms."

She laughed and sat on the edge of the bed. "No. They're the type who'd trade a horse with the glanders and expect boot."

"You poor girls must have it hard, always protecting your virtue."

"Well ... yes and no. It's fun sort of, unless the guy is a rat, won't take no for an answer."

"Then it's always no?"

Her good healthy laughter rang out again. "Mostly ... Now you shut up or you'll find out what a loose woman I am and hate me."

"I wouldn't hate you but I might date you ... poem."

"Say that's good. Oh, that's right you're the author. I read your stuff and brother if you can love like your characters ..." She rolled her eyes and shivered convincingly. She was a little overblown but she was within bounds and delightfuly curved. Every move she made suggested sex, clean wholesome sex. Not the eye fluttering, chirpy, middle wiggling kind whose every act was a singboard, but a healthy emanation that came from her like the breath of expensive perfume.

"Tell you what, when I get up let's go eat a big meatly meal some place."

Her eyes shone. "Goody. I've been hoping you'd ask me. You're not like the people around here. You're cute and you're a celebrity. I'd never stop bragging about going out with you."

"And I'll promise not to make you walk home."

"That's a deal." She stood up, arched her back and looked sideways at him. "I'll be waiting so don't disappoint me."

"Promise. Just as soon as a little necking won't rebreak my ribs."

She laughed again and whirled out of the room. He lay back and asked himself why he had made her the promise. On the other hand why not? In his mind a picture of Ferris formed, the poignance of her delicate features, the smudged starlit outlines of her young breasts, her shyness after boldly showing them to him. Did he owe her loyalty? Not yet. Later maybe.

Back at the plantation Berry was facing a new problem. Mart had a visitor. Berry's reaction to the fact not only shocked and surprised him but made him furious with himself. What Mart did was none of his business ... then he saw that she was cold with rage. The man was a big lumpy brute of a fellow dressed in Mississippi-Texas style or what the average soda-jerk cowboy thought was the last word in range wear. Levis that clung to his thick legs, cheap gaudy boots with fancy stitching and square toes, and a cream colored hat rolled sharply along the side. His left arm was hung stiffly in a black silk sling and he seemed to favor it although it was not in a cast. He stood with one foot on the low back porch and spoke in a low confidential voice to Mart who leaned against the wall of the kitchen near the door, her face pale and tight with distaste.

When she saw Berry she relaxed and a look of relief came to her face. Berry, now hypersensitive to unspoken emanations, still angry at himself, strode purposefully toward the casual figure of the man.

Six feet away he stopped and Bud Kitchen turned slowly and gave him a lazy smile. "Mawnin'."

"Who're you," asked Berry unhospitably.

"Me ...? I'm Bud Kitchen. You musta heard of the Kitchens. Just thought I'd drop by for some cawffe ... or sumpn." He leered and looked back at Mart who chose this moment to turn abruptly and disappear into the house.

Berry's feet were widespread and his eyes dangerous. "Mart, come out here."

She came to the door. "Sir?"

"I said come out here."

She came out and stood stiffly at the edge of the little porch. "Yes sir."

"What's *this* doing here?"

Bud's face flushed. There was no mistaking the insult in Berry's voice.

"He came here with a proposition I want no part of. It includes him and me in a situation I'd rather be dead than submit to ... with him."

Berry lunged and at the end of it a big right hand lashed out and Bud Kitchen rolled on the grass. "All right get up and get off this place and if I catch you on it again there'll be more of the same."

Bud sat up groggily and worked his jaw. "You're new here."

"So what?"

"You'll learn the hard way, bastard."

Berry stooped, yanked the big man to his feet like a block of hay and the right shot out again and again Bud Kitchen measured his length in the grass.

"That's for free," said Berry tightly. "Get up and get out."

Bud, hugging his left arm close to his body got up then leaped. Mart screamed a warning and Berry side stepped the rush and the slashing right hand that held a knife commonly know as a Texas Jack. Bud whirled but Berry's left foot traveling with all the power of a big hard thigh smashed into Bud's stomach and for the third time in less than two minutes he dug his face into the grass. Berry picked up the knife in a rage, broke it and hurled the pieces afar.

This time Bud took some time before he could even sit up so Berry caught him by one foot, dragged him to the red pickup in which he had come, opened the door and threw him bodily into the truck. "Just put a foot on this place again," said Berry, "and you'll get it worse."

This time, Bud, his usually florid face as pale as skim milk, was in no condition or state of mind to argue the point and as soon as he could gather his shattered equilibrium he started the truck and drove slowly away.

Back at the house Berry spoke to Mart whose face was still wooden from the experience. "It won't happen again," he said gently.

She shook her head. "It will happen again. It follows me wherever I go."

He studied the quiet nobility of her lovely face and marveled at the purity of its lines. Never, he thought, had he seen such placid inherent beauty. Her skin was the color of sun ripened apricots ... and smoothed. Her eyebrows were thick stygian bars of unpluckered richness, her eyes ever so slightly oblique, and almond shaped. They grew damper as he studied her and finally overflowed. "I can't stay here and cause you trouble."

"What will you do, go home and have them after you every time you put a foot out of the house?"

"That won't get you in any trouble."

He frowned heavily and his jaw hardened. "What sort of a bastard do you take me for? You're not going any place."

"Don't make me stay," she whispered twisting her hands together. "I'll only make trouble for you."

"But I don't want you to go … I won't have it. Do you think I could sit here and know that you were being mistreated and maybe manhandled by a bunch of dogs like those Kitchens …?"

Her eyes opened a little wider. "Why, sir?"

His jaws clenched together again. "Because …" He stopped, appalled at his traitorous mind. It was a parallel emotion that he had felt when he saw Bud Kitchen talking so confidentially to her. He shrugged angrily and brushed past her headed for the living room and thought her eyes were still wet, a ghost of a smile hovered over her perfect lips.

CHAPTER SEVEN

B erry's visit to the hospital the next day was not a gesture for which Ronald was grateful. His brother had been in a surly uncommunicative mood and his presence wandering around the room looking out of the windows and replying to questions in short sentences was an irritation.

Later, around noon Charley Olsen came by with a tremendous tray which outstripped the previous one. It was loaded with fried chicken, rice and rich brown gravy, hot buttered biscuits, green beans and the most delicious cornbread Ronald had ever eaten. In spite of his sore ribs and generally low spirits he was so loaded by the time he came to the peach cobbler with thick cream that he was miserably full when he finished.

He sighed as Charley took the tray away. "Do you people always eat like this?"

Charley grinned amiably. "Well, a feed like that is sorta special but mostly we have it once a week and at Christmas and maybe Thanksgiving. We eats pretty plain 'cept when there's a reason not to. Plenty, mind you, but plain. Lots of vegetables like peas and okra and corn and butterbeans and snap beans ... the pole kind. Them bush beans ain't fit to eat. Same's butter beans. Calico butterbeans is the only kind to eat. Them little green things they call limas ... Shucks! 'Course there's 'taters too. Irish and sweet. We eats Irish 'taters more like a vegetable and not every time you turn around like the yankees does. Plenty of good biscuits and cornbread too. People turns up their noses at fat back too but if its good side meat with plenty of lean it's fine for breakfast and other meals. We eats a lot of pork in winter and some beef in the summer but mostly it's chicken and a good bit of fish. We get 'em from the Gulf and plenty of people catch bass and perch and cat and freeze 'em down. I reckon 'cept for a few ignorant tenant farmers we eats pretty good."

"I reckon you do," said Ronald burping discretely.

"Hear tell your brother had a brush with Bud Kitchen."

Ronald started and grimaced with pain. "I'll be damned. He didn't say a word about it."

Charley Olsen looked uncomfortable. "Me and my big mouth. Maybe he didn't want you to know."

"The hell with him. What happened?"

"Seems like Berry come home and found Bud there trying to get Mart Patterson to go to the bushes with him or something. Seems Berry didn't like it too much and cuffed Bud around some. Bud's in here now."

"What?"

"Yeah. Said Berry kicked him in the belly. Had a hemmorage and the Doc had to go into him to stop it."

"If Berry kicked him," said Ronald, "then he had a good reason. Kitchen must have tried to pull a gun on him."

"More likely a knife. Bud carries one of them Texas Jacks … but it weren't in his duds when he took 'em off for the operation."

Ronald's eyes narrowed. "How do you know?"

Charley grinned. "I got ways. Beats all what a man can come onto when he's got ways."

Ronald nodded. "Ever blackmail anybody?"

"Nup … not for money, that is. I mind the time I used some little knowledge I had on Dil Adams. He was ranting and cussing something terrible because his daughter up and married Bill

Mark's oldest boy ... the one what's in the Army. Dil was all for shooting the boy or doing him some such damage and I had to quieten him down a little."

"How?"

"Well, Dil's got a few low down ways, too, but I'll give it to him, he tries to make up for 'em. He's got a few off color woods colts running around, spite of all the moral airs he can root up when he's a mind to, so I told him to sorta cool off 'cause I didn't think he'd care for people in general to know about that there family he's supporting in the next county. Even sent the three oldest to some college in Alabama."

"Did he cool down?"

"Considerable. Simmered off and now that the gal's got a couple of fine kids and the boy made a commission on the field in Korea and got a coupla medals he's plumb 'shamed of himself."

"What are you around these parts besides Mayor of Tide," asked Ronald, a gleam in his eyes.

Charley squirmed. He had talked past his intentions and his extrapolitical activities always made him uncomfortable when they were known. More often they were not.

"Well ... I looks around and gives a hand here and there. Man's lifetime is short and I think he ought do what comes to his hand."

"It says so in the Good Book."

Being a man of much curiosity and having traveled extensively Ronald had become inured to shock to a considerable degree but nothing in his past had sufficiently toughened him for the blow that followed him home from the hospital.

She must have followed him because he had hardly been deposited sweating from pain and tension in his bed when a car drove up outside and a vision climbed forth, assaulted and carried the house on the first charge. Brushing Berry and Mart off as thought they did not exist she stormed into Ronald's room and covered his astounded face with kisses and tears.

"What have they *done* to my darling," she crooned throatily as she stroked his face with her hands contriving at the same time to stroke his chest with the points of her sharp breasts.

He pushed her away gently, furious because of the storm she excited in him. "Madelyn, for God's sake stop it. No one has done anything to me and I'm not your darling. I'm not even your husband any more."

Her deep blue eyes flooded with tears. "Ronald, can't you forgive and forget?"

She was still trite, he noticed. She had a full store of phrases to fit given situations and other than those her vocabular y was meager. He had often told himself that she would be a good teacher of basic English because it was all she knew. There were times when her pat sentences did not quite fit the subject and the effect was often ludicrous.

"I had forgotten rather successfully until you barged in again. What the hell are you doing here?"

"Why ... didn't you know Merle Potter is my cousin? I was paying her a visit and heard you and Berry had moved down here. Then we heard you had been hurt and in the hospital. Was it very dreadful darling?"

"Oh nuts," he snarled. "It was wonderful. What happened to all your lovers?"

Her beautiful face grew doleful and her eyes drooped sadly. "Ronnie, you can be cruel you know."

"I know," he said distractedly. "Look, I'm a sick man who mustn't be disturbed. Beat it will you?"

Tears again. He cursed under his breath because the sight of them as it always had made him squirm and feel like a dog no matter what the cause. It stimulated his guilt complex.

She leaned forward sitting on the bed letting him get a good glimpse of the rich shaded depths revealed by the low neckline of her dress. Also a thigh had escaped its cover and shone with a dull glow. He contracted all over and winced as his ribs pained him. She still had the power to upset him and as of old never missed the opportunity of using it to the full. "I'll go Ronnie but I'll be back. Oh Ronnie, you know how I love you."

He laughed gratingly. "I know well enough. What was the jerk's name I slaughtered in the apartment that time?"

She shook her head slowly. "That was so long ago," she whispered.

Berry, after Madelyn brushed him off left the house in a state of mingled rage, chagrin, and a tinge of unease. He had never liked her even when she and Ronald apparently were very much in love but he had always been conscious of a sneaking fear of her.

Mart reacted differently. This woman was a rank foreigner ... just who she wasn't certain but whoever she was Mart did not fear her. Instead she had conceived an instantaneous and active dislike for her. That she was beautiful, tall, distinguished and *soigne* to a degree Mart was too honest to deny. This same honesty disposed of these points as unworthy to stand in opposition to her dislike.

In the bedroom Madelyn walked up and down dramatically presenting the case of the unwanted wife. "It isn't as though we were total strangers," she declaimed. "Just look what we once had ... the love ... those wondeful nights, the moon ..." She stopped because Ronald had uttered an obscenity.

"I remember what we had. You running the show from all angles. When I wanted to write you wanted to go places and be seen, dog shows and God knows what, stage entrances like a deistic visitation. Any idea I ever had become yours after a decent interval."

She fell forward on her kneese and clutched his right hand in both of hers. "But Ronnie, I've changed. I don't want to run anything. I just want to be loved."

"Oh hell ... Look, I've asked you in a nice way to get the hell out. Do you want me to call the help?"

"The help has arrived," said Mart implacably standing in the doorway. "I think I heard the gentleman ask you to leave."

Madelyn stood up and surveyed Mart through chilly eyes. "Who," she inquired, "is this?"

"She's Mart, the housekeeper."

"A delightfully arranged tart, I must say."

"Whatever you have to say you can say somewhere else," said Mart tightly. "He said you go and you go. Erect and walking or face first. It doesn't matter to me.

Madelyn smiled like a dragon about to pounce. "What delightful help you have Ronnie. What do you depend on her for besides bouncer? I can't think of a cozier arrangement ..."

She stooped because fingers like steel sank into her wrists and she was almost hurled through the door into the living room where she caught her foot in a rug and pitched sprawling. Livid with rage she leaped to her feet only to be expeditiously ejected through the glass door leading out on the veranda. She stumbled and just managed to avoid falling again. Then the true Madelyn burst through her carefully applied lacquer of sweetness that had cracked visibly when Mart came into the room. She now burst into a flood of the most obscene vituperation either Mart or Ronald had ever heard. Mart snapped the night latch on and strode away, her marvelous hips rolling with a slightly exaggerated motion that delivered a last insult to the raging Madelyn.

Without an audience Madelyn gave a final scream of fury and walked around to the back where Merle Potter waited in her car.

Ten minutes later Mart walked silently into the room and looked pityingly at Ronald who had thrown an arm across his eyes and was perfectly still in bed.

"That you, Mart," he asked without moving his arm.

"Yes sir. I just wanted to say how very sorry I am."

"Forget it. She was my wife, once."

"I thought that must be the explanation. I'm glad it's in the past tense now."

He took his arm down and regarded her through eyes that were soft with affection. "Do you always take other people's troubles to your heart?"

"People I like."

"Then you must like Berry and me because every time something pops around here you're right there to try to put it right."

"I think I cussed somewhat."

He smiled. "Better than that. We haven't mentioned that night out there but I'll never forget it. It was the only thing that held me together. You must have known that."

"I think I did. I don't regret it for a second and I'll be there again if you need me."

Her eyes did not waver under his intense scrutiny. "I don't think I ever knew a person quite like you before."

"It's unlikely that you have. I think I'm a pretty special person."

Laughter came easily to his lips now. "Sit down, Mart. I want to talk."

She sat down and for an hour he rambled. When he had finished she knew his life history, three dimensional.

Her face was a study in calm placid beauty. Never had he seen such serene perfection of feature, such utter control and yet there was no suggestion of woodenness or immobility. "I told you you'd tell me some day."

"And you were right, of course. Tell me, Mart, what will happen to all of us?"

She sighed. "I wish you hadn't asked me that."

"Why?"

"Because I happen to know what will happen and all of it isn't good."

"Like what?"

"There'll be more trouble with the Kitchens. Mr. Berry will kill one of them or they'll ambush him and kill him." Her deep dark eyes swept back to his. "May I tell you something I hardly dare believe?"

"After what I've told you? Anything you say is locked up."

"He's in love with me ... but I don't think he knows it yet."

Ronald laughed with relief. "Mart, that would be a shocking statement to some men I know. To me it is so far from being a shock that I'm actually relieved. However, that sort of thing down here won't be fair to you."

"That's where you're wrong. If I love him and he loves me and we have each other what else should I want? Mink coats and a long car?"

"You should be able to have children. You can't ... or you won't."

He felt like pulling up the sheet to protect himself from the light that seemed to shine from her.

"Mr. Ronald ..." She got up and on her lips was a smile of such utter beauty, of such courage, of such power that Ronald tensed all over. "Mr. Ronald," she repeated. "That's something else you're wrong about. I'm the illegitimate child of a white man and I'm *glad* I'm alive."

Bud Kitchen was resting better than he had any cause to and had even become fly with a couple of nurses. He was no particular friend of Charley Olsen so he was understandably short with the Mayor when the latter paid him a visit. Bud was no better friend of the Mayor's so the interview was brief and to the point.

"What you want," asked Bud short temperedly.

"Just want to give you something for free," said Charley twirling his hat on a pudgy forefinger.

"Must be advice," sneered Bud.

"It is. Better not horse around over on Little River no more," Olsen's blue eyes were hard. "Reason I'm telling you this is not because of any great love I got for the Kitchen family. Just that I hate to see good people inconvenienced ... and I ain't talking about the Kitchens. It might put Mr. Berry to some worry to have to let light through your belly but he's the sort what'll do it."

Bud sneered. "That damn yankee ..."

"That damn yankee," said Charley softly. "However, that ain't exactly what I was driving at. It just might make me a little sore too. Them fellers I took to first time I laid eyes on 'em. Wouldn't consider it a very friendly act if you boys give 'em any trouble."

This sort of talk Bud could understand. He could also understand the flinty hardness of Charley's usually mild blue eyes. Talk was that Charley had killed a couple of people during his tenure as marshal and the usually bad Kitchen boys had trodden warily as long as he wore the star. Now that he was mayor they still respected his influence and kept their distance.

"I uster hear a saying," pursued Charley, "that when the oldest man of a family met a sudden death the others was likely to go the same way. Jeff Kitchen was shot through the head trying to ravish a man's daughter." He nodded wisely and his eyes were still hard as he turned to leave the room. "Better think it over," he said as a parting shot.

Bud sweated a little, glowered at the white ceiling and began to plot.

CHAPTER EIGHT

Twilight was beginning to purple the eastern horizon. Ronald sat up carefully and breathed the balmy air that swept through his open window and considered the recent past and the future.

The latter seemed obscure and doubtful, the former fraught with fear and pain. He thought of his interview with Dr. Blackwell and felt better. It was up to him, Blackwell had said. He grunted heavily and gasped as a bright sliver of pain lanced through his side.

The twilight grew darker and night sounds began to drift in with the quiet breeze. The woodland symphony was as old as time itself and yet he knew he'd never tire of it. Then like a sprite who formed a part of the naturalness of the tableau Ferris trotted down the path by the bluff. She wore tattered old shorts that had once been khaki pants, and a white T shirt. He noticed with a stab of feeling that the shorts were something less than the bare minimum for modesty.

For a reason which he could not explain he didn't want to see her. Even at the time he realized the utter stupidity of any such feeling … recalled the shattering kiss she had given him … all the wonder of her body, the direct frankness of her deep grey eyes … every quality about her and still he felt a freezing revolt at the thought of seeing her.

He called Mart with all his might and in a matter of seconds she stood in the door.

"Don't let her in here," he panted frenziedly. "I don't want to see her ... Please Mart ... don't let her in."

She surveyed him coolly for a moment. "I'll do no such a thing. She is a wonderful child and don't think I don't know why she comes. It isn't for meat alone. I never saw anyone so concerned about you when you were in the hospital. Mr. Berry even offered to take her to see you but she was afraid to be gone that long."

He fell back in bed defeated and as soon as he knew he had no choice he grew calm. When she walked in, her eyes shining and her face bright with gladness, he was almost normal ... but not quite.

She stopped abruptly and a spasm of pain flitted across her face. "Oh, Ron ... aren't you glad to see me ... really?"

"Damn," he muttered. "Am I that transparent."

She came to the side of the bed, her lips trembling. "I don't understand," she said after regarding him for a moment. "Why do you have to make believe with me? I'm your ... friend. I think I am anyway."

"You are, kid," he groaned. "Probably the best friend I have. I've got worms in my head and I've never been more truthful in my life when I say I don't know why I didn't want to see you. Now that you're here I'm glad as all get out. You'll stay for supper won't you?"

She sighed. "I don't know. The look on your face when I came in made me feel awfully funny. I was all prepared to see you smiling ... and you were but it was all cracked up and lopsided."

She sat down and looked at him, a matter that he found vastly disconcerting.

He said very distinctly. "Ferris, I'm glad to see you, as glad as a man could be to see a woman."

She shook her head slowly. "If you were in love with a woman you'd be gladder to see her."

To this there was no immediate answer and he floundered badly, then spoke stupidly. "How do you know I don't love you?" He could have butted his head against the wall for that question.

Her face lighted like a beacon for a moment then the light died. "If you loved me you wouldn't take that way to tell me about it."

Ronald forced a laugh. "Look Ferris, it's a little early to speak of love, don't you think? I think a lot of you and that night when you kissed me it shook me all the way to my toenails. Let's not get precipitous here and spoil something that may be the most wonderful thing that ever happened to us."

Tears collected on her abnormally long dark lashes, "I'm just an ignorant country girl," she said in a low vibrant voice. "I don't know anything but what little I've read … and what my heart tells me. The time for me to say I'm in love is when I feel it. I don't know anything about being precipitous … I don't even know I was being that way." Her head went slowly from one side to the other.

"You haven't said you loved me, Ferris."

She stood up like she had been shot. "I know I haven't *said* it aloud but your're a man of the world, a wise man who writes wonderful books. Don't you know?"

He was struck dumb and realized that he was alternating his big feet in his big mouth, one after the other.

She leaned over him, her hair sliding over her shoulders and framing her face closely.

"I love you, Ron. There, I've said it. Now maybe you hate me but I've said it. Not because you asked me to but you told me I hadn't. Don't ask me how much because everytime I think of the tremendous feeling of it I almost burst. I can't find any words to describe it."

She was gone and Mart was at the door. "Supper is ready. Will you try to make it or shall I bring you a tray."

Feeling that his chest was about to explode from the power of the forces built up by Ferris' visit he sat up giddily. "All right, raise hell with me."

"Why should I?"

"Don't stand there and tell me you didn't hear everything that went on."

"I won't, but I fail to see what comment I'm supposed to make."

"I do too," he replied wearily. "Maybe nothing. I just thought maybe you would."

"Shall I?"

"By all means."

"I think you're being immature. Maybe you always have been. You had a spell of maturity during the war and you performed nobly. Since that time you've been slipping backward into childhood. Your repartee just now, your whole conversation was childish. Not wanting to see her was childish because she represented a problem ... just why, is somewhat obscure since she is obviously so in love with you that just listening to her made me ache with sympathy. You'd have known a long time ago except that you threw up a wall of resistance ... no one knows why, and shut your eyes to the truth. What better time to tell anyone that love exists than when it is known?"

"Has Berry told you he loved you?" He said resentfully.

"No, he hasn't, but Mr. Berry is a mature man. When he realizes it he'll tell me. Of course, he fights the obvious too. I think most men do, else they fall flat and blubber out a declaration of undying love and feality but they're worse than those who are a little careful. I could have laughed aloud when you asked for it and got it. How does it feel?"

"Like hell. Please go away Mart. You're not being very sympathetic."

"Oh, but I am. Just not with you. I'm in sympathy with her."

She was gone and Ronald got up and put on a bathrobe, tying the sash with a vicious snap of his wrists, pinching his belly painfully. Pain … pain in everything he did. He felt like crying for a moment then good sense came to his rescue temporarily and he forced a short macabre laugh.

Berry was surly and uncommunicative at supper, bending a little toward the end of the excellent meal to discuss cattle.

"The Kitchen's have been in the herd, or ten fat calves and seven good cows have fallen in a hole in the ground."

"I didn't see any holes that big the day I went exploring."

"I didn't either. Cole and Abe Marks, they're Bill's boys, found where the fence had been cut and a truck driven in."

"That ought to cinch it. Any tire marks?"

"They're not that dumb, the tires are so slick they don't make any marks."

"That ought to be just as good."

"It would for me, but not as evidence that'd stand in court. A lot of trucks have slick tires."

Ronald lit a cigarette. "What do we do, stand guard?"

"No. We sit and wait. While we're waiting we'll brand everything, ear mark 'em and tag 'em."

Ronald eyed his brother critically. "You've been as sour as a bear since that Kitchen affair."

Berry's eyes came up slowly. "What Kitchen affair?"

"The one you didn't tell me about."

"If something happened and I didn't tell you about it then it is safe assumption that I didn't want to discuss it."

"Okay. I was just wondering."

"You don't look too hot yourself."

"I'm anything but hot. Every time I make a move it's loaded with trouble. I run off bluffs and into women I can't handle."

"Who ... Ferris?"

"Ferris. She's a problem."

"How's that?"

"She's in love with me and if that isn't enough Merle Potter turns out to be Madelyn's cousin and the minute she hears where we went when we left Toledo, here she comes panting with declarations of feality and devotion. I could have shot her this afternoon."

"Me too. Think she'll be back?"

"I don't know. Anyone else I'd say no ... the way Mart bounced her, but you never know what Madelyn'll do."

Merle Potter was stringy, freckled, orange haired and forty. Her husband had left her a big plantation and a fat bank account so that now all she had to do was ride on the momentum he had set in motion. She was a good manager, had a number of good colored and several white families as tenants so her future was assured. In one thing Ronald had been wrong. It had not been Madelyn who made the discovery of their move but Merle, who had written her cousin after she discovered the identity of the new owners of Little River plantation. Madelyn had replied to the letter by packing and taking a train.

They sat on the cool shaded veranda of the old plantation house and Merle listened while Madelyn stormed and blew.

"Darling, I think you're all stewed up over nothing. If he doesn't want you then I can't see what you can do about it."

Madelyn's eyes narrowed "I can tell what a coward he was in Korea."

"That didn't get the publicity his medals did during the war."

Madelyn almost whimpered with rage. "That dirty *bitch* who threw me out of the house. He's probably sleeping with her. *She's* the one I'm going to get."

"How?"

"I don't know ... but I'll get her."

"I'll let you in on a secret. I know some men who might help."

Madelyn leaned forward. "Who?"

"The Kitchen's."

"Who're they?"

"Four brothers. They steal cattle, make whiskey and run after women ... and they're the most fascinating men you ever met."

Madelyn was interested. "Tell me more, Merle."

Merle giggled and blushed. "Well, it isn't easy ... you know ... after being married and all, then to have no husband ... and I'm not as handsome as I once was. Now you're not to tell a soul this, but they make whiskey on my place."

"They do?"

"Yes. As my part they let me have good whiskey that's aged and I put it in labeled bottles and serve it. I drink it too. You've been drinking it since you came."

"Why, that's perfectly good whiskey. In fact I like is better than a lot of the brands on the market."

"That's what I think. It saves me a lot of money."

Madelyn stole a sly glance at her cousin. "Is that all you get?"

Merle blushed again. "You might as well know since you'll meet them and if I know you ... well ..."

Madelyn shivered discretely. "What're they like?"

"Peas in a pod. Big, husky, handsome, red faced boys, with sandy hair ..." She stopped and giggled. "They also have a heavy covering of shiny body hair. Bud's chest is like a bear rug. Berry Summerville nearly killed him the other day because of the woman who threw you out of the house. He's in the hospital and for a while it looked bad for him."

Madelyn sneered. "Berry is a great ugly brute of a man. A sour puss who never liked me. Does Bud want the woman?"

"They're very frank about such things. He wants her in the worst way ... probably because she won't have anything to do with him."

"Humph, she should be flattered."

"She isn't and its got him burning. He's burning over another girl that lives next to Little River. She's the daughter of some cranky ex-professor. They live with old Ben Macklin ... he's a nut. I've never seen her but Bud talks about her all the time. He tried to take it a couple of times but he hasn't succeeded yet. He will. He never gives up on something like that."

"Merle, I'm inclined to think you're a bitch."

Merle laughed throatily. "Aren't we both darling?"

Madelyn giggled. "It must run in the family."

"It does. What about a drink?"

"Wonderful but I'd better warn you, when I've had a drink I want a man."

"Only then? I can promise you one. Ruke and Alex are running off a batch this afternoon. We'll pay them a visit, and if Alex doesn't offer to take you swimming then discover that neither of you have swim suits, I'll drink the whole batch alone."

Madelyn shivered and hugged her breasts. "Let's make a move. First the drink, several maybe, then swimming ... or something."

"*And* something. Tell me darling, what do you see in Ronald Summerville, anyway?"

Madelyn's eyes narrowed. "I see his bank account, dearie. Anything he writes sells like mad and although he hasn't written anything in a couple of years his stuff still sells wildly in reprints and that's where the money is. I used to make him hop through hoops before and I'm going to do it again. I'm going to move into that dream house and move Berry out. He'll go rather than to live with me."

"I wouldn't be too sure about that. Your first attack was not a signal success."

"The drink darling, the drink. Strategy will be needed."

CHAPTER NINE

By the end of the week Ronald was up and around, still breathing softly favoring his cracked ribs but able to take walks and suffer in his choice of locale. As long as he suffered physically his mental pains seemed a little remote but now that he was on the mend Madelyn's visit began to plague him, when and if he would stop thinking about Ferris ... and she was no small problem.

Today he had subconsciously taken the path leading to the creek where he had watched the near ravishment of a woman who at the moment meant more to him than any on earth.

For a moment he remained in a state of chill immobility then Berry rode into the clearing and seeing Ronald, dismounted. "What're you all frozen up about," he asked.

Ronald pointed a shaking finger. "Snake," he croaked.

Berry grinned. "I didn't know you were afraid of snakes."

"Not afraid of little green garter snakes, little snakes ... but that, that's a monster."

Berry walked to the log and as he did the snake slithered off into the grass, apparently in no particular hurry. Berry reached down and gently picked up the beautiful reptile. It was a glossy shimmering black sprinkled with greenish white spots. It seemed in no way put out and while Berry remained still it crawled up his arm and took one turn around his neck and directed its beady eyes at Ronald who was practically in shock.

"King snake," explained Berry. "Old Bill showed one to me the other day. He and his boys keep 'em in their corn crib. They eat rats. Non poisonous, almost tame. Did you notice, he didn't even offer to bite me."

Ronald passed a trembling hand over his brow. "Aren't you going to kill him?"

"Hell no! Never kill a king snake. They kill and eat rattlers and moccasins. This one's so tame I believe he's the one Bill and I played with down by the creek the other day."

Ronald grabbing his courage in both fists got up and approached his brother, a wary eye on the big snake.

"Want to hold him for a while? Be good for your morale."

"No. I definitely don't want to hold him but maybe I'd better if I'm going to stay in these parts. Don't rush me, now. Let me take my time."

"Just be gentle with him. Here, hold your arm out and let him crawl from mine to yours. I gotta go get the Marks boys to help me with a couple of dehorns."

Forcing himself, with very instinct in his screeching for flight he let the cold slithery reptile crawl slowly from his brother's arm to his own, his flesh corrugated with horror.

The snake semed suspicious too for a moment then repeated the process of crawling up his arm and taking a turn about his neck. Ronald almost fainted.

"He'll be a big pal of yours," said Berry getting back on his horse, "When you're through just slide him into the grass. He likes your neck because it's warm."

For the better part of half an hour Ronald steeled himself to the snake's advances and at the end of that time he found the courage to handle it deliberately. Never had he seen such cold serpentine grace. Each scale seemed to glitter, like a black jewel and the white spots on close examination appeared a light yellowish green.

He sat on the log and placed the big snake beside him but it showed neither fear nor inclination to flee. Instead it crawled across his legs, doubled back and regarded him with black beady eyes. "Suppose," began Ronald conversationally, "you just crawl off and get lost some place."

There was no change in the beady eyed stare.

"I think I'll call you King. Doesn't that flatter you?"

If King was flattered he gave no sign of it. He did crawl off Ronald's legs and wind around a branch slithering up to shoulder level where he composed himself as for a long vigil.

"Exactly what goes on in a snake's head? Are you in love with anyone? Do you have trouble with relations, sour milk, dental caries or do you fluoride your water?"

With a whipping flash King snapped down from his perch. So suddenly did he move that Ronald suppressed a scream of fright with difficulty. He leaped to his feet and stood on the log then he could see the reason for his new friend's precipitous action. Coming across the path headed in the general direction of the log was a rusty cotton mouth moccasin, ugly, venomous, his triangular head moving sinuously as he slithered forward. Then he saw King, snapped back into striking position and waited. King moved toward him with a slow deliberate crawl then turned aside as though to pass and did draw several inches past the moccasin's head then like a flash of light turned and struck. Immediately behind the big head King buried his teeth and the two snakes instantly went into thrashing action that only ended when King had the moccasin so wound up in his coils that the latter couldn't move. Tighter and tighter grew the constricting coils and Ronald could hear the soft pop of joints, either from King, from the pressure he put into the embrace or from the moccasin for the same reason. The latter's mouth was open now and his long fangs erected themselves momentarily then sank back. Tighter and tighter grew the glistening black coils until at last it was obvious that the victim was either unconscious or dead. King released his grip on the head and nosed about a bit until apparently satisfied that there was no further action to be expected, then opened his fastidious jaws and took a big mouthful of snake head. With a wriggle of his jaws that somehow reminded Ronald of a cootch dancer's motion, he engulfed the entire head, his jaws spreading widely to admit the piece de resistance. For a long time Ronald watched with fascination as King gradually engulfed the meal, a fraction at a time. As he would swallow an inch he would release an inch from the coils which he had not once relaxed until finally there was only enough of the tail left to afford support for one coil and even then he did not release the grip until his nose was pressed against himself. When the meal was finished King rested motionless for a long time then crawled sleepily away into the brush.

Ronald laughed a little and went back to the log where he sat until twilight began to dim the brilliance of the soft afternoon air and the nightly musical efforts of natures nocturnal children started.

He started back and stopped as an exhuberant rush of music struck his ear. Someone was scattering delightful notes from the big grand piano and they had a blythe racing enthusiasm that did not speak of Berry's half hearted fingering.

Was it Chopin? He decided it was not. This was melody, repetitive in a sense and yet he knew it was not the repetition of passages or notes but a style that ran over and over itself seeking and finding hidden grottoes of tone, dallying around them then dashing away with light fingered joy, seeking and finding others.

His heart pounded heavily when at last he looked through the glass front of the house and saw Ferris, her right foot leaping over the padals. Her feet were bare and her legs glowed in the soft light that shone from overhead. His stomach knotted when he noticed the proprietary smile on Berry's face and the way he hovered over her as she played. The knot tightened as he saw her face tilt upward and smile at his brother.

He turned slowly, and went to the big cedar tree and sat in the outdoor chair. His breast churned with emotions that made him ill. Being jealous of Berry was unthinkable but since when, he thought, has jealousy been put to flight by logic.

If I'm jealous, he argued, why do I shrink from any talk of love with the kid. Kid … that was it. She was too young. He felt absurdly pleased at this neat bit of mental prestidigitation … then angry that he could be capable of so palpable a bit of self illusionment. Right out of a clear sky something occurred to him and made him feel light and happy. He had feared the king snake with the wholly unreasoning fear so many men have of snakes, yet he conquered it and forced himself into a friendship with the reptile. At last he had conquered a fear. He bounced from the chair and strode with long strides toward the living room just as Ferris poured herself off the piano stool, stood erect and walked toward the kitchen with Berry's arm lightly over her shoulders. She had been laughing again, her face turned up to his. Instantly Ronald's lightheartedness disappeared and the ache came back but he snarled aloud, "If I can play with a snake, I can do anything."

They were already seated by the time he had washed up and were deep in conversation about music when he took his seat.

She looked up. "Hello, Ron."

"Hello," he said tightly and attacked his soup.

"You should have heard her play," bubbled Berry enthusiastically. "She played for half an hour and it was all improvisation. Marvelous stuff really. I've been telling her she should try to get it down with the idea of publishing it."

"What makes you think I didn't hear it?"

"Well, did you?"

"I heard it. It was grand."

They exchanged looks which he saw and it made him feel bitter and left out of things so he withdrew into a shell of silence and as soon as he finished eating he got up and went to his room.

"What," asked Berry with a sigh, "are we going to do with him?"

Her face fell and she sighed tremulously, "Berry, what does one *do* ... really? Do we actually help when we try, do we provide incentive, or do we do it by threatening, begging, bribing ..." She shook her head. "I don't know but I do think we're probably trying too hard. Maybe we should give him time. I'm sure he needs it."

His eyes were soft with admiration. "I'm sure of something, too, kid. You're the luckiest thing we've had happen to us in a long time. Things that are as obscure as a thunder cloud to a lot of people are as clear as a blue sky to you. I think you put your finger on the trouble with us. We want too much to happen too fast."

Her eyes dampened. "I'm worse than you. I pushed him and frightened him when I shouldn't have. I know that now but I didn't at the time."

"You're in love with him, aren't you?"

"So much," she half whispered, "that it's killing me. I want him all the time with an intenseness I can't even calm down. It happened, the first time I saw him ... like a cord breaking, instantly and I went all mushy inside. Berry, there'll never be anyone for me but Ron ... not ever. I know I'm young and maybe pretty stupid about worldly things, maybe underdeveloped emotionally but I was never surer of anything than I am of that. Tell me, does he have any feeling left for his wife?"

"Always speaks of her as his ex-wife," said Berry quietly. "I couldn't tell you for sure what he feels but I do know that you knocked him for a loop the first time just as he did you. Man is a funny creature about things like that and the better his case moves along the more likely he is to hedge. The thought of losing you would drive him into action quick enough.

She sighed. "Maybe I'm asking for too much but I don't see it. Why do people fence like that when often their happiness depends on it."

He laughed shortly. "That's a good question. Why do men hurt the women who love them? Why do women hurt their men? Man is God's chosen creature but he can certainly climb the heights of asininity at times. That's why I could never believe that man was made in God's form. Man is supposed to be able to reason and look what it gets him."

"May I comment on that," said Mart from the sink where she had been quietly washing dishes.

"Of course," said Berry warmly.

"Reason when it can be divorced from impulse and emotion of various sorts has a chance of being something usable. When it can't it rarely shows its face."

Berry chuckled. "We should record all this profundity, Worse philosphy has been written and sold for good money … Then you divorce love and reason completely, Mart?"

Mart showed her white teeth in a smile. "I didn't do it, but it happened. Find a couple really in love and try to tell one of them something snide on the other. They'd both climb in your hair and if it happened to be the truth their reactions would be stronger than ever because they'd have probably had some subconscious realization of it already and be quicker than ever to go on the defensive. That's why every man and woman who ever fell in love thought they had discovered each in the other something *different.*"

"And," put in Ferris, "they can hardly ever explain what that difference is. I know I couldn't where Ron's concerned.

❧ ❧ ❧

The next day the telephone company produced the service they had been promising for some time and for Ron came the first call. Mart summoned him from his room where he lay staring in a carefully compounded state of blankness. "The phone for you. It's a lady."

He sat up with a groan. "If it's Madelyn ..."

"It isn't she. I'm not familiar with this voice."

Ronald levered himself off the bed and was pleased to note that his side seemed to have improved a great deal since his walk of the day before. He went into the living room and still wondering, picked up the receiver.

"Hello."

"Mr. Summerville?" Silver bells, throaty silver bells ... gold ones maybe.

"Yes."

"This is Carla Peterson ... your student nurse who piloted you through the dark tunnels that approach the dismal labrynth of death."

He flushed heatedly as he recalled a passage he had written which, if her remark did not duplicate, it was close. "Well ... how's the girl."

"No author should be trite," she flipped back. "Couldn't you do something better than that such as the feed you promised to buy me?"

"I shall be especially careful in the clinches. I promise."

His reaction was at the same time one of dismay and a strange anticipatory thrill. "What are your days off?"

"Today is one. That's why I called you. Since my home is in town I don't have to be back before seven tomorrow morning."

Again the chill attacked the sensitive skin of his back. "When do you have to be home?"

"That," she said with softly lowered voice, "will depend on too many things to discuss here."

"I was afraid of that."

She laughed. "When can I expect you?"

"Where shall we go? I'm a stranger here, remember?"

"Well, it's thirty miles to Meridian. They have good eateries there."

"Then we'd better start early."

"Right. I'll be ready at three so we won't have to hurry."

"Three ...?"

"Sounds good to me. Too early for you?"

"Well ... I guess not, but ... All right. Where'll I pick you up?"

"At my house."

"I gathered as much, but unfortunately the whereabouts of your house isn't known to me."

"Oh, I'm a little thick. Must be anticipation. Remember the street the courthouse is on?"

"Yes."

"All right, my house is the first house on that street ... the west end of it. Has square brick pillars and a cape jasmine hedge leading from the front gate which has 'The Petersons' written on it in wrought iron."

"I dig you, kid. See you at threeish."

Ronald cradled the phone and stared numbly at nothing. He was frightened out of his wits. What did this brazen woman mean to do to him? What were her plans?

She came tripping down the winding stairs and she was a sight that made him forget his flippancy and catch his breath.

Something very sheer in light blue that complimented her eyes and clung to her lush curves revealing the necessity for underclothing to maintain a modicum of propriety, revealing frail straps across her shoulders and across the hips the faintest stripe that moved, as she walked suggesting the hem of some breathless gesture of underthing.

"Aren't we fine ones," she said smiling so brilliantly that he felt a little search, "ambling off in mid afternoon."

"That was your idea. By the way, your're a somewhat different person out of uniform."

"Somewhat different … you'll have to do better than that. I'm hideous in uniform."

Still casting at each other they were ushered out of the door by her smiling mother and like adolescents they were still kidding fatuously as they drove off.

She gave him a few short directions then leaned back against the seat and sighed. "I didn't believe I could do it."

"Do what?"

"Wangle a date with you. I'm shameless about things like that. When I want a date with a guy he has to practically knock me down to get out of it."

"I wasn't that hard."

"Hard enough. Why did I have to call you?"

His face tightened a little. "To begin with you may think you have a bargain but you don't."

"What's a bargain?"

"Don't be foolish. You know what I mean. I'm all loused up … practically psycho. I'm all cut up inside and out. Three drinks and I'll either weep, get confidential and maudlin or retire into a shell like a spoiled brat."

"Maybe you are one. It's something to think about."

"I have and maybe you're right. Do you like people like that?"

"No."

"Then why're you out with me?"

"Because all you've said can be put under the heading of self-diagnosis. Dr. Mayo when he gets sick goes to another doctor. Self-diagnosis isn't worth a toot. Keep talking and I'll have you pegged in a moment."

"I don't know whether I'd like that or not."

"Ah, then you admit the dope you're handing out is guff?"

"I didn't admit ..."

"You did too. I say I'll peg you, you say you wouldn't like that, so what you said is a smoke screen. Elementary, my dear Ron."

"Smart cookie, aren't you?"

"Not smart but not a dummy either. Say, you've carted me five miles and nary a pass or pet."

"Are miles an indication of such?"

"Not exactly. I thought my fatal charm would work long before now."

He laughed. "You throw me every time I open my mouth. Sometimes when I don't. I'm afraid I don't know when you're being serious and when you're kidding."

She slid over and caught his right arm, pressing one firm breast against it. "Smart author takes lessons from hayseed nurse. Want me to tell you how to find out?"

He glanced in the rear view mirror then ahead. No cars were coming so he pulled over to the side of the road and stopped. He did not need to offer much in the way of offense because she met more than halfway and her lips sent his mind into a dizzy torrid whirl. They were soft agile things that seemed to melt and pour over him in a torrent of aching sweetness. Against him her breasts were softly distorted but throbbing with the unsteadiness of her breath.

One of his hands slipped carelessly over her dress, hesitating momentarily over one elegantly peaked erection. Her breath stopped dead in her throat, her frame tightened convulsively and a frenzy seemed to overcome him as he attempted to read the reaction.

Her head slowly moved from side to side. "Please Ron ... don't push me over." It was a breathless whisper.

He could hear some stupid voice asking, "Why?"

A sad little smile twitched the corner of her lips. "Because I'd rather not have it that way. Because maybe ..." A sob seemed to contract her throat. "Because maybe I think I deserve just a little more consideration. Don't you?"

Never in all his life had Ronald been so softly yet effectually shattered. "Of course," he said huskily. "If you don't deserve better treatment than that then no one ever did."

"Why do you say that? Maybe you don't agree with me.

"It just happens," he said getting the car under way again, "that I do agree with you. Just charge that scene back there to ... Well, the fact that a son of a bitch and a man sometimes look alike on the surface."

A soft hand closed over his. "I don't want you to feel that way. What if I told you I want just what you want?"

He let a bursting sigh go and felt foolishly relieved. "Carla, many a man has been fooled by what he thought was a come-on, but what I love about you is that you didn't go into the usual female routine of 'What sort of girl do you take me for' and other such weary cliches."

"Ron, you still don't understand, do you."

"No, I guess not. I'm pretty thick today apparently."

"What makes you think I wasn't as eager as you back there?"

"Because, swine that I am, I'd have kept on. You made me stop about as gently as I ever remember anything happening to me."

"You're getting warm. Let me put it this way. I'm not as young as my looks and years might make me seem. What we just stopped can be wonderful … or it can be cheap and sordid and a mere flicker to be forgotten. I don't want it that way. Now do you understand?"

"Maybe I'm beginning to. You mean you're not a first date opportunistic sort of girl."

"No I don't mean that. Look let me make you a promise, then maybe you'll get it. Before we get home tonight we'll do anything you wish."

His hands grew sweaty on the wheel and a vast ache welled up in his throat. "You don't have to make me any such promise."

"I know that but I made it anyhow. Now do you see what I mean?"

"Maybe I do … I don't know. I'm afraid to guess any more. You're a frank kid. Go ahead and tell me."

She shook her heavy blond hair over her shoulders and nodded. "All right, I'll tell you. I'll draw you a picture. The first time I saw you and found out who you were I wanted to have a date with you. I've dreamed about it and every dream ends the way you'd like it. What do I care about first dates? You're not a kid who'd go blabbing about how easy I was to make. You're different. I'm not the usual type as you've been kind enough to tell me. I'm dragging it out and I'm stopping … right now. I want you too Ron but I want you *right*. I want it to be something wonderful, not something that happened ten minutes after we left the house on the side of the road on the front seat of a car."

He nodded heavily. "Well, I couldn't say I don't understand now. Why do you, a comparative kid have to give a suave well traveled intellectual, a lesson in taste?"

"You're being unnecessarily harsh on yourself. You had an urge and you followed it. I had a similar urge but I want it to be done differently."

He shrugged hopelessly. "Look, Carla. I know nothing about this country. I know nothing about the way you want things except what you've told me. I couldn't arrange a decent ... whatever you want to call it, if my life depended on it. Tell you what, from now on the ball is yours, take it and lead me wherever you want to go. If I don't lead well, kick me where it'll hurt."

Her young face lighted with a smile. "It's not considered becoming in a girl to do that sort of thing but I'm the kind who doesn't care. Keep going, fella and I'll call the turns."

He never knew why he blushed.

She deftly changed the mood and all the way into Meridian she lead the conversation in light, amusing, unimportant chatter for which he felt vastly relieved, taking as it did some of the sting from his earlier action. He found, however, that she was a creature of moods that changed with dynamic suddenness. Deep in the parking lot at a swank roadhouse they got out, taking a swift glance around she went into his arms and again his ears thundered to the power of her touch. For a long moment he seemed to swim in a veritable well of sweetness, satin soft, moist and trembling then she drew away her eyes shining mistily. "That was nice."

"You have a flair for putting things very simply."

"Most things are simple. We love to make them very complicated in order to make ourselves appear deep and complex. A kind of wish fancy as a sop to our ego."

"Let's go eat. This racketing vacillation between Heaven and earthy philosophy is making me dizzy."

After the bountiful meal and crystal thimbles of *creme-de-menthe* and ice they smoked and talked about nothing serious.

"See what I mean by a feed outside the white walls once in a while?"

He grinned. "I noticed you put that steak away with a dispatch equal to mine. Aren't you afraid for your figure?"

"Yes, I am, but not from the eating point of view. It's a little over the svelte minimum but don't you think that's all right?"

"What can I say when you've read my stuff?"

"You avoided that trap neatly enough. I fit the girl Darlene, the expatriated German girl on the loose in a mid-western town because her husband hadn't given the correct address don't I?"

"Perfectly ... even to the hair and eyes."

"Shall we go or do you wish to blot up a few more unlawful Martinis?"

"I don't care for any more Martinis but if we could have a bottle for the road ..."

"I shall press the miracle button and you'll see a mysterious package forthcoming."

The package was forthcoming and at a service station they bought chasers and sallied forth in the direction of Tide.

Some ten miles from town Carla sat up. "I begin leading you astray. Up ahead there is a gravel road to the left. Take it."

"To where?"

"To Chatafaw River and my brother's camp."

"Where is the brother?"

"Far far away buying appliances. Chicago, I believe."

"You wouldn't have a father or other brothers likely to come down on us?"

"I have both, but one, the father wouldn't go to a camp for money and the other, a brother, younger than Jake who owns the camp, is with Jake in Chicago. Any other questions?"

"Yes. Why are you doing this?"

"Because we both want it. Can you think of a better reason?"

"Nope. I guess not. I repeat you don't have to just because of the promise."

"That objection I have already answered and I will not repeat myself."

They drove for five or six miles winding gradually lower until they crossed an old steel bridge its gaunt framework rising over the decking in weird geometric figures. Below the sand stretched whitely away from the stream proper that was catching the first rays of a bloated summer moon.

"On the left is a narrow sort of trail, a road you could call it … Oh oh … you missed it. Back up."

He backed up and directed the car down a road that was grown up with weeds in the middle and on both sides.

They burst suddenly out of the forest that cloaked the road on both sides into a clearing in which was built a rough but roomy camphouse with screened porches. It faced the river, and the front yard dropped off suddenly onto a white beach.

He stopped beside the rough iron rock chimney and got out, going around and opening the door for her.

She went into his arms again and this time, with nothing to interfere they remained close for a long time. Her breath fluttered as she drew back a little and smiled. "Still want me to run things?"

"No," he replied gently. "I think I can carry on from here. Shall we knock and enter?"

"Just enter. Here's the key."

"You came prepared."

"I tried to tell you that but I ended up having to draw you a mural."

The house was roughly furnished but comfortable and Carla built a tiny fire in the rock fireplace out of packing boxes. "It's small and won't give out much heat. I love fires. They hypnotize me."

The kitchen was big and hung with huge iron pots with heavy lids. "Things taste better cooked in pots like these," she said. "We'll have to come out some night and cook up something."

They made a drink and drank it then another, bringing the second round back to the big central room that was bunked with double deckers around the wall serving both as a living and bed room. Carla had lit an oil lamp when they came in and now she turned it down until it was only a dim yellow glow. In the fireplace flames licked upward bathing them in a ruddy glow.

They sat on a hand made couch that he had dragged before the fireplace and now they sat and sipped their drinks watching the flames.

"Thanks to you," he said at length, "I feel relaxed for the first time in a long while."

"That's nice," her voice soothed him like fresh cream on hot skin. He put his emptied glass on the floor and reaching over pulled her to him. Fire flashed in his brain as their lips touched and his nerves thrummed to the certainty that this at last was what he had waited for.

Her body was quiescent yet strong … strong for the end they both sought. Her breasts bared now for the tasting were satiny cups of the purest texture and the song in her throat as old as Eve … The moon hung low and cast a gleam of golden light across the room, striking her soft flank and gleaming metallically off her hair. Her face was soft and ethereal in the half light as she snuggled closer and sighed with gentle relaxation.

"I knew it would be this way," she said breathing into the curve of his neck.

"I didn't," he said, his voice threatening to break on the corners. "I had no idea …"

"There will be other times, Ron."

"Yes, there will be other times."

"Let's not confuse this with love … please."

"Are you against love?"

"No, and I think really this is by far the greatest thing about it but ... I don't know. Maybe I'm afraid I'll run you away or something. I do know I feel very close to you. I don't suppose we could make something frighteningly beautiful like this and not feel close. I'd just like to know that it will go on ... under it's own momentum. Of course, one day it won't but I'd like to think that even then there'd be no exhibition of temper or bad taste and a loss of friendship."

He squirmed slightly. He wished she'd get off the subject. She was exhibiting a bazarre attitude and of late he had met nothing but women with bizarre attitudes. That any women could be as brutally objective about something that had but a few moments ago been objective only in nature's blind way was something that shook him sorely.

"Don't you agree with me?"

"Yes," he said slowly, "I agree with you but I wonder where you found the ... whatever it is to turn the usual female attitude so completely into reverse."

She snuggled closer and the renewed sensation of her exciting body, clinging to him from throat to instep, sent blood thundering in racing cascades again. "There's an old Mississippi saying that you should never look a gift horse in the mouth."

"I doubt that it originated in Mississippi," he replied dryly, "but it's a good saying ... and I won't. It's a little bit fantastic and I'll make you a bet."

"What?"

"This may not be your first time but it was damn near it."

She was silent for a while. "You're the third to be exact. I've been in love, Ron. and maybe that has something to do with the way I feel about this. I was in love at seventeen and he was a lover all right up to a point. He didn't have a lot of trouble making me give. I like to give when I want to. I wanted to but it was nothing like this. Maybe I was too young or maybe he was too young. It only made me want him more. He just never seemed to realize that there were two people involved.

He nodded understandingly. "Who was the first."

She smiled. "A little boy of twelve when I was ten and we were both frightened to death. Even then I knew that it would be something big in my life some day." She kissed him with lingering sweetness. "Like tonight."

Her eyes were starry when she looked into his. "Ron ... do my eyes look like yours?"

"Yes," he said throatily, and drew her into a fierce embrace.

CHAPTER TEN

The next morning Ronald, coming from his shower headed for the breakfast room, came face to face with himself, something that was a shock of noble proportions. He was some years younger but in size, physical conformity, the resemblance was stunning.

"Hi, Uncle Ron." They gripped hands hard.

"Tommy! Where'd you come from?"

"School. Got in a little trouble. I was tired of school anyhow."

"Seen your father?"

"Yes sir. A few minutes ago. He romped on me some but ... Gosh, Uncle Ron this is the most wonderful place I ever saw. School ..." He spat the word out and leaned forward eagerly. "How about you and me putting the pressure on him. I want to stay here."

Ronald patted the boy's shoulder. "You can depend on me, kid. We'll talk it out of him."

It was later, breakfast almost done, before Tommy brought the subject up. "Uncle Ron and I think I ought to stay, Pop. I never saw a place I love like this. Woods, fields, streams and it never gets too cold."

"You and your Uncle Ron, besides being peas in a pod, are nuts" said Berry dispassionately.

"Naturally," said Ronald." Only an artistic nut could appreciate fertilizer piled as high as Berry Summerville."

Tommy stifled a laugh. "What about it Pop? I could help with the cattle and ride a horse. Gosh, I just thought of that. Think of riding everyday."

Berry frowned. "What about your college education?"

"I told you, I got kicked out."

"Why?"

Tommy flushed and looked at his cup of coffee. "A small matter of *l'amour* that had a little bad luck."

"Well, Prof. Luker came home unexpectedly and caught his only Angela in a slightly disheveled condition and naturally drew harsh and unreasonable conclusions. I was not able to satisfactorily explain a certain rumpled aspect presented by myself and I was invited under the circumstances to either get hence or get hell. I took hence."

Berry's eyes narrowed. "You not only look like your Uncle Ron, you flap your jaws in a certain abandoned manner which passes this day and time for intellectual patter. Let's hope you don't have his flair for getting into trouble ... But that's a wan hope in light of what you've just said."

"You talk about us flapping our jaws," put in Ronald, "but you still haven't answered the kid's question."

Berry looked frowningly paternal. "Well, you'd both remind me that I had no education to speak of and look what a golden example I turned out to be so ... Okay, but by God you'll fork that horse till the sight of hair'll make you ill. You'll learn to rope, hogtie, brand, castrate, dehorn and the rest ... and while you're at it you might as well round up the rustlers that've been stealing our cattle."

The boy's eyes gleamed. "No kiddin' ! Real rustlers?"

"Real ones. I can even give you their names, the Kitchens. They make whiskey and steal cattle."

Tommy showed his white teeth in a grin. "They can't be too bad if they make good whiskey."

Berry looked at Ronald with alarm but the brother only laughed. "College wasn't like that when we were boys. Times have changed."

Berry shook his head. "Seems just like yesterday he was blubbering and snuffling because he had taken a dive off his bicycle and skinned his knees."

Tommy flushed. "Aw, I didn't do all that blubbering."

"You did enough. This morning we've got a cow to find that should have dropped a calf last night."

"Have you a ... er, sorta gentle horse ... You know, for a starter?"

"I have a roman nosed roan that's as mean as a tiger. No sense in starting at the bottom of the ladder."

Tommy looked dubious but brave. "Well, he can't do anything but kill me."

When they had gone and Ronald was sitting in the living room, he remembered the boy's last remark and applied it to himself. At that age nothing frightened him. Now everything did.

His hands were wet and he scrubbed them on his trouser legs. He had overcome fear of the snake ... but when you came right down to it, what danger did the snake offer? A nonpoisonous snake that his brother handled safely.

By this mode of thinking the one courageous thing he had done slipped from grace and the wells of blackness tried again to engulf him.

Charley Olsen drove up in drab coupe and climbed out laboriously followed by an individual as spare as a rail but very erect. The tall man wore a black dust streaked hat and at first glance Ronald thought he had a toothache but closer examination revealed the lump in the cadaverous face to be tobacco. He spat copiously as he followed Charley across the lawn.

Ronald met them out on the front veranda. "Morning Charley … Come in."

"Morning Ron. This here is Sheriff Sam Williams."

"Hod do," said the sheriff, extending a limp hand that went steel hard when it closed over Ron's.

They took deep comfortable chairs at Ron's invitation, then Charley launched into the purpose of his visit.

"Seems as how a woman's done come to visit with Miz Potter. Says she usta be your wife."

"That's correct. She came here and I had her thrown out of the house. She hasn't been back."

"Well, she's been in mighty bad company, I'll tell you. Running around with them Kitchens ain't likely to do her reputation no good. Thought might be you'd want to know about it."

Ronald said. "Can't say as it makes a lot of difference, Charley. I'm divorced and glad of it. I have no idea why she came back down here."

"Claims she still loves you."

Ronald frowned. "How'd you get in on this?"

"Well, she and Alex Kitchen was riding the other night and run over Ab Perkins' Red Poll bull so Ab called up the sheriff here and had 'em took in. Said they was drunk. Alex was for a fact but Miss Madelyn didn't seem too drunk. I took her back to Potter's but Sam kept Alex in the jailhouse until the next morning when he got bail. The Kitchens is pretty hot over it."

"And you talked to her?"

"Yeah, I went down there … Sam had to push Alex around a little to get him locked up and I went over to see what the ruckus was. We had a little talk."

"I suppose you told her what she was doing to herself."

"I did but somehow it didn't ring back."

"How do you mean?"

"She done some blubbering and stuff and got strung out on how bad she been handled and how she still loves you but you're a hard mean man. What I said seemed to register all right judging from all the water it brung forth but I didn't seem to catch none of it. Didn't ring back."

"I see and I salute your perception. Madelyn can turn on tears like out of a faucet."

Sam Williams leaned forward and spoke, his voice a soft throaty drawl. "Them Kitchens is been on their way to trouble fer years. Knowed it when I first took office fifteen years ago cause their old man was a demon if there ever was one. I will say for him though, he had guts. These boys don't 'pear to be overloaded in that department but them's the real dangerous kind. Ole Efe woulda stood up and shot it out with a man he didn't like, in fact he done it several times till Jess Appelby let light through his brisket one evenin' with a London Twist loaded with scrap iron."

Ron stared at the sheriff then at Charley. "I know you two didn't come to ask about my wife. You must have something on your mind."

"We is" said the sheriff. "A week ago a family from upstate come down and squatted on a little place back in the woods what the Kitchens owns. Turns out they's old Efe's brother's family. Three boys, the mother and a coupla girls. I hear tell it got too hot for 'em upstate so they ducked out quiet like. Point is, that makes three more in addition to the four Kitchens what we got here. Come to my mind that we's overloaded with two branches of the same breed of dawg."

Charley said, "Since you and Berry is the ones they might be sore at right now, we thought we'd better tell you to be on the close watch. Them sort of people like to shoot from cover."

Ronald felt a chill of icy fear. "You mean they'd bushwack us ... just like that?"

"Just like that" said Sam Williams grimly. "The main thing I want to tell you boys is this. Them people is knowed all around fer whut they is. If you'd come on 'em takin' your cows or something like that and smoke 'em up, you'd get off with a clean bill. That's a nice way of putting things right. On the other hand if you ever walks up on 'em stealin' and ain't armed they might be a missin' person for me to worry over. One what'd never be found. There is it. Fer's me and Charley sees it either you get them or they'll get you. Go on and pack your guns and hope they don't get you first."

"I'd like for Berry to get in on this" said Ron, in the cold sweat of fear. The idea of getting potted at every time he poked his nose out of the door was not a pleasant thought.

Berry obliged by coming around the corner of the house. "Caesar threw a shoe ... Oh, hello, Charley."

He was introduced to Sam Williams and listened while Sam gave him a gist of the situation.

"We'd damn well hate to lose two good citizens", he continued, "and as you can see there comes a time when the law is like a one-legged man at a broadjump match. Them boys is sharp and they's dangerous cause they ain't gonna come right out and shoot nobody. They's the bushwackin' kind."

Berry's face was hard. "What exactly do you advise us to do?"

"I advise that you get yourself a coupla good rifles and some side arms. If you don't wear 'em keep 'em handy. Get yourself some saddle scabbards fer the rifles. I don't mind admittin' in private that the way I'm set up, until they is caught red handed in their devilment or I get enough evidence to stand up in court there ain't a thing I can do but sit and hope some citizen catches 'em and smokes 'em up."

"What," asked Berry, "would happen to the citizen?"

"People'd clap glad hands" said Sam shortly.

"Madelyn," put in Ronald, "was picked up last night with Alex Kitchen. Alex was drunk and had run over Ab Perkins bull."

Berry's eyes went hard. "I always did say she had the morals of a mink. Did you lock her up, Sam?"

"Nope. Don't like to lock wimmen up. The jail ain't exactly a rose, you know, and after all she wasn't all that soused and was just ridin' with Alex."

"Well, I'm glad you fellows told us what to expect. We'll be as ready as we can."

Ronald was too ill to eat the noon meal. His stomach had knotted up so badly after the talk with Olsen and Williams that he was bordering on funk.

He sat at the table with Berry and Tommy and fumed. "I thought I left war in Korea and damn if we don't buy a plantation right in the middle of it."

"Chance" said Berry.

"Hurray" said Tommy. "I can be a cowboy and wear a .45 Colt in a low holster."

"Can you hit the ground with one" asked Ronald.

"Sure. I took three years of R.O.T.C. and having an uncle as famous as you I hadda make good range averages. I got expert with pistol and sharpshooter with rifle."

Suddenly Ronald realized that Tommy was one person who didn't know of his cowardly flight in the war zone ... and it is just as well, he thought. Youth always *defied* courage.

That night after supper Ronald went out and stood at the edge of the bluff, standing a safe distance from the edge, and took stock ... as the thought was phrased in his mind, of nothing.

"Lookin' fer Sally" said Unker Ben absently. "Been lookin' fer her a long time but she don't never show up. Musta met with some foul play. I seen Sam Williams about it but he didn't seem to care one way or t'other. You promised me you'd sorta keep a lookout fer her."

His presence calmed Ronald immensely after the first shock of his appearance. "I've been thinking" said Ronald, unable to think why he was saying such a thing, "Ferris looks like Sally, doesn't she?"

"Spittin' image" said Unker Ben, massaging his dry hands together.

"Maybe Ferris is Sally. Maybe Sally died and came back in the form of Ferris."

Unker Ben's eyes looked at him for a long time with a blank uncomprehending stare, then he turned and walked away muttering. "Somebody else told me once that Sally was dead. If she died how come somebody didn't tell me about it?"

Ronald felt ill, thinking he had done the wrong thing. Why had he suggested such a thing to the old man?

He leaned against a small gum tree for a while looking out into the purple depths of the valley then he sat and rested his back against the bole.

He recovered consciousness after a time and immediately got up and went back to the house.

Berry sat at the piano toying with chords and Tommy poured intently over a western goods catalogue.

Berry looked up and stopped playing. "Oh no, don't tell me you fell over the cliff again."

Ronald shook his head and stumbled to a chair. "Snake" he croaked breathlessly. "I was sitting under the gum tree and that king snake crawled up in my lap. I didn't know it was there and when I looked he was coiled in my lap looking at me. I think I passed out."

Berry turned back to the piano, knowing that nothing he said would help matters any, his mind troubled more than was obvious. He was certain that his brother, instead of improving was growing worse. He seemed to be aimlessly working toward nothing. His actions were sporadic and seemed to be performed on the spur of the moment and not a day passed that he didn't have to endure some dreadfully frightening experience.

Ronald got up. "I'm going to bed."

CHAPTER ELEVEN

He tried to relax but didn't succeed. He thought of Carla ... and understood Mart better. He thought of Ferris and felt the knife twist gratingly. The knife went deeper when he looked out across the lawn and saw her walking hand in hand with Tommy, both laughing and intent on the others' face.

He sank back in bed and suffered. Youth, looks ... his own, almost. What little trouble it would be for her to transfer what she felt for Ronald to Tommy. Youth and courage. A lad whose life was ahead of him Ronald felt his own, sere and barren and intimidated, a personification of age. Thinking on the subject drove him to breakfast not hungry, not wanting to eat, but determined to be there and watch them. Maybe he could tell.

"Good morning, Ron" she said sweetly.

"Good morning. When did you two meet?"

"Yesterday afternoon" put in Berry. "I haven't been able to get any work out of him since."

"It was late" said Tommy defensively, "and on top of that her father ran me off."

"He ran Ron off too" said Ferris taking a sip of orange juice.

"He figured Uncle Ron was too old for you" said Tommy attacking his eggs.

Ron, who had told himself the same thing times on end felt a sudden blaze of rage which he quelled instantly.

"He is not too old, any such" said Ferris coming to his aid. "He's not at all old."

"You must be doing all right, Uncle Ron," said Tommy rou-gishly. "How's about telling me how you work it."

"Eat your breakfast, we've got work to do," said Berry with such shortness that Tommy gave him a quick searching glance and devoted his attention to eating.

The rest of the meal proceeded in relative silence with Ferris eating three eggs and a ham steak of some size, relishing the last bite. Ronald pecked about and ate little feeling that the world had turned black.

After breakfast when Berry and Tommy had gone to look for a young calf suspected of having screw worms in its navel, the latter with manifest reluctance, Ferris cornered Ron on the veranda. "Ron, you look and act sick."

"I am," he declared shortly.

"Do you want to tell me about it?"

"No."

She was silent for a while and he had that sick feeling in the pit of his stomach that always came when he knew he had hurt someone unnecessarily.

"Ron, have I done something you didn't like? I mean like the day you came back from the hospital. Maybe I seemed too anx-ious or something. I didn't mean to hurt you or make you angry."

He closed his eyes for a minute fighting the acute agony she set up in every fibre of his being. "No Ferris, you haven't done anything. It's just like I told you. I'm a dud, a wrong number, a fizzle, I'm off the beam … way off. If you pinned me down I couldn't tell you what the trouble is except that abject cowardice of mine. Alex Kitchen knocked me off the steps at Merle Potter's last night. I ran, shaking all over like a wet dog. I hurt you without wanting to because you are another complexity that I'm afraid of. I can't think normally when you're around, and the only refuge I have is to keep my mouth shut … and ignore you, maybe. That's not the way I want it at all. Maybe I'll get over it."

"You don't sound convinced … not even when you're trying to convince yourself. You're not a coward, Ron. No coward would admit it so freely. It is something that you'll whip. I know you will. It's foreign to you or else it wouldn't make such a frightful lot of difference. A coward is accustomed to the state and had a full store of compensations both from within and without."

His eyes, glazed with misery swung aroung to hers. "I watched Bud try to rape you and didn't even have the guts to help you."

Her face blurred so he missed the swift wave of compassion that swept over it. He only heard her words. "I'm so very sorry, Ron."

When he could see clearly again she was gone and so was most of him. He sat in a semi-dazed state for a long time, unable to think because he so earnestly desired not to. She was sorry for him … palpably just something to say to ease the utter contempt she felt. Yet the voice had seemed soft and understanding. She was that sort and she had not had time to let the full enormity of it reach her. He felt suddenly frantic, like a man whose nostrils are only an inch from the water and his movement is downward. Like the frenzy of futility in a nightmare … a train is thundering down the tracks and the dreamer cannot move.

Later that day, Berry and Tommy came in, washed, dressed and departed for Meridian where they purchased two .30 Springfield Sporter rifles, saddle scabbards, a quantity of ammunition, three .38 automatic pistols and shoulder holsters. Thus armed they returned home with that feeling experienced only by an unarmed man finally getting his hands on a good weapon and plenty of ammunition.

One particular morning after having sat for an hour and a half after breakfast he got up and wandered off toward the back of the house again automatically taking the path that led to the creek.

He reached the creek and noticed immediately that another person had walked the sand bar not long before. He stopped and studied the tracks but could tell little about them until in one place the sand was damp and he saw the perfect print of a cowboy boot. Instantly without thinking that both Berry and Tommy now wore them, he thought of the Kitchen's, cringed and hid behind a sweet laurel bush. For sometime he peered downstream then he saw.

Samp Kitchen was huddled close to the bank of the stream half hidden by an overhang of alder bushes. He moved and Ronald could see the glint of a rifle barrel. Ronald went cold and white, his hands shaking violently then he turned and ran quietly back upstream. Four hundred yards up the slope he found the two Marks boys and Tommy holding a small group of mixed Brahma and Herefood cattle under a spreading magolia tree.

"Where's Berry," panted Ronald as he ran up.

Tommy straightened in his saddle. "Good gosh, Uncle Ron, you look like you're about to crap out."

"*Where's Berry?*"

"Down the hill there bringing up a cow and a new calf. What's the matter?"

"Down the hill there ... in the creek. One of the Kitchens with a rifle. He's hiding."

Tommy started then with a curse slid from the saddle and snaked a beautiful new Springfield Sporter from his saddle sheath. "Is that a fact, now, he said metallically.

"Jeff, you and Luke stay here and hold this bunch. When Pop comes tell him I said to stay here. Come on, Uncle Ron, and show me."

"Want us to go too," asked Luke, his mild blue eyes now hard and eager.

"Thanks … no. This is a family affair. Come on, Uncle Ron."

"What'll you do?" asked Ronald, his face dripping with the sour sweat of fear.

"That'll depend," said Tommy snapping a cartridge into the chamber of his rifle with a practiced flick of the bolt. "He'll need a good excuse for hiding on our place with a gun."

After ten minutes of careful walking they crossed the creek bed and keeping under cover they approached the hiding man directly from across the creek and behind. When they reached the sand bar he was covered only from the front and upstream. Ronald held back when Tommy with a low growl of satisfaction leaped from the low bank down to the sand. His voice whipped the still air like a lash. *"Turn around, Kitchen."*

The thick bodied man turned all right, but he turned shooting. The bullet went high whipped past Ronald's face digging bark of an iron wood and showering him with stinging splinters.

Tommy's weapon smacked the air with a crisp clear crack and Samp Kitchen tumbled backward still clutching his rifle. He rolled to the edge of the water and turned over bringing up the muzzle of his weapon as he did so. Again the Springfield spoke with authority and this time the big man sank to the sand, his red head falling backward in the water. He shuddered a few times then went lax and still.

Tommy snicked the safety of his rifle. Pale and tense walked back to the bank and held up his hand for Ronald to give him a lift. Ronald did so, hardly having the strength to pull the boy up.

"What ... will we ... do ..."

"We'll go tell Pop, then he can call the sheriff. He fired first. Remember."

"He fired first," said Ronald mechanically and began to pluck splinters from his face.

Two hours later they all trooped back down the hill. With the sheriff was the coroner, a dumpy little doctor with a tiny black mustache and a wrinkled seersucker suit that was yellow with age, and Charley Olsen, his big face red with exertion.

The sheriff walked in the lead apparently knowing where he was headed, his long legs setting a good pace. He was lean and tireless and the walk hadn't even made him sweat.

They waded the creek at the shallow place oblivious of their shoes and soon were in a rough half circle around Kitchen.

"Old Samp," said the sheriff, breaking the silence. "Had t' put him under a peace bond once. Threatened to shoot Wade Mulkey 'cause Wade whaled the rear off'n Bud in high school. Seems as though he sorta took over when old Efe died. Made the boys hop but always took up fer 'em. What say, Doc?"

The doctor got up from his cursory examination. "First one took 'im through the upper right thigh. Second one went in just under the right clavicle ..." He shook his head. "Big, thirty caliber ... didn't come out. Muster churned up his lungs and guts into ..." He shook his head again. "Like a bucket o' clabber toted muleback. Couldn't a died no instanter."

Sam Williams took off his big black hat and patted his grey locks into place. "Tommy, y' say he fired first?"

"Yes sir. I said 'Turn around Kitchen'. Well, he turned, shooting. I shot as fast as I could and he fell backwards and tried to take a bead on me again, then I shot him again."

Sam Williams grinned. "Got him both times." He turned to Ronald. "Mr. Summerville, how did you come t' see him like you did?"

Ronald, his belly a slab of ice, unstuck his tongue and said in an unnatural voice. "I was just walking. Had thought of taking a swim but when I got to the place I felt like walking some more. I could hear the boys up on the hill hollering at the cattle and I had half my mind on them. Then I saw one of those yellow boots sticking out of that clump of bushes there. I hid and watched until I could see he had a rifle. Then I ducked out and went up the hill where the boys were."

"You wasn't armed?"

"No. I didn't expect any trouble ..."

"Then I don't blame you for taking out like that. Good sense."

Ronald looked away, feeling the calm eyes of Charley Olsen on him as he did so.

"Well, said Sam Williams pawing his colorless moustache. "Looks like that's it. Plain case of self defense. Samp woulda had a time explainin' how come he was here hid on the creek bank ... on Little River Plantation armed with a thirty-thirty. 'Specially when Mr. Berry here roughed Bud up some."

Charley Olsen chuckled. "Yeah ... Some! Pink Parson comin'?"

"Yeah, I tole him to follow us. Him and Hamp oughta be here pretty soon." He turned to Tommy and put a paternal hand on his shoulder. "That was a good piece of work, son," he said, "but you're in a spot. They'll be gunnin' fer you and your pa too now."

Tommy gestured with the Springfield that he still carried. "I'll have this."

"You may not be lucky enough to get the advantage again. Just be on your toes and don't take no chances."

"I think this'd be a good time to pull up and take off," said Berry his face white and set. "I didn't think we'd come into a feud the first month."

Every face in the little group was turned on him and for a few seconds there was a dead silence.

Sam Williams was as inscrutable as a sphynx. So was Charley Olsen. The pudgy little doctor wore a tight half smile that might have meant anything. Ronald's face was relieved and Tommy's incredulous.

"Do *what*?" he blurted unbelievingly.

"Get out!" said Berry harshly. "Scram! Think I want you killed before your ears get dry?"

"A man does what his conscience says do … much as he can," said Williams gently. Then added, "I guess."

Tommy spread his feet and gripped the rifle hard. "Well now. I don't get this and I want no part of any tail turning. Let the sons of bitches come. Dammit, Pop, that's the first time I ever heard of you wanting to pull up and scoot because a dog barked at you. Well, go ahead. I'm staying."

Charley Olsen looked at Sam Williams and saw that he also had a desire to cheer wildly. Neither did because at that moment Pink and Hamp Parsons and four husky Negroes came through the bushes behind them. After a short discussion they loaded the body on a collapsable stretcher and the Negroes lifted it and started away.

At the house Mart served coffee on the veranda and spiked Charley Olsen's heavily with Martel brandy.

He tasted it, his face went blank then broke into a smile. He glanced back over his shoulder intercepting Mart's glance and smiled. She smiled back. From some past meeting she remembered that he liked black coffee and brandy.

"What can we expect from the authorities, Sam," asked Berry, still icy hard and pale.

Sam smiled a little shamefacedly. "When I talked to you about it the other day I mighta made it a little over simple because I'd forgot that the District Attorney is sorta related to the Kitchens. Don't know how he feels about 'em but he might try to bring it to the Grand Jury. That won't make no difference. The thing is too plain and like I said he was on your property."

Charley Olsen spoke up. "It's like he says, Berry. It could come to the Grand Jury but even if it does it won't amount to nothing."

Tommy sat a little back from the older people his face as hard as his father's and his eyes burning hotly. Ronald sipped his coffee and said nothing.

Sam Williams put his coffee cup carefully on the stone floor, "Well, we better be goin'. Son," he spoke to Tommy. "Play it close to home for a while and watch your step. If they even crooks a finger at you do your trick over just like you done it today."

Tommy nodded. "I'll be all right."

Sam grinned. "Somehow I think you will too."

When they had gone Berry turned to Tommy. "So you're for sticking it out … your neck I mean."

"If that's what you want to call it. They were after you today, not me."

"They'll be after you now."

"You too."

"What difference does that make?"

Tommy stood up, his feet a little apart and the very air about him was charged with the courage and bullheaded belligerence of youth. "Okay, run if you want to. I wasn't built that way and I didn't think you were either." He turned and disappeared into the house.

As he passed through the living room her voice arrested him. "He was doing it for you, you know.'"

He blinked. "Well, so what? He needn't do it for me."

"You're not a father and can't be expected to understand just what it means. However, you seem intelligent enough. You should have some imagination."

"Maybe I have but I'm not running like a whipped puppy."

"That's beside the point. The point is, don't feel badly toward him because he wanted to do something to protect you. When he beat Bud Kitchen I told him I wouldn't stay here and cause him trouble. I thought then he'd beat me. If you think your father is a coward then all I can say is, you're a fool."

He stared at her incredulously for a moment then laughed. "Thanks for reminding me. For a moment I must have gone a little foolish. Of course he isn't a coward. Exactly who *are* you anyway?"

"I'm just the housekeeper. Just like yesterday and the day before."

He went to her, a little overwhelmed by the golden loveliness of her lithe graceful body and the placid force that shimmered in her face like the subtle shock of heated iron on a bright day when the redness is not visible but the heat is. He touched her lightly on the shoulders and his hands felt like they had touched high voltage. "You're guilty of some awful understatements you know."

Her smile dug deep in his vitals. "Thank you, Tommy. You're a sweet boy."

"Boy ... and today I killed a man."

"You killed a dog. There's a difference."

"Thanks again. I'll think of it that way and it won't bother me. You may bother me, however."

Again the sweet smile that was a trifle sad. "I didn't hear you but I'll answer that. Of course, I'll bother you. You're human."

He shook his head. "I don't get you at all. You always make me feel sort of little boyish. I thought that remark would get you. Instead you make it sound like something ... well ..."

"It's hard to explain, but I know what you mean. You say I may bother you. I may. Maybe you'll return the compliment but I don't think you will."

"Why?"

Her face was like Mona Lisa's. "Can you take a shock?"

"I think so."

"I love your father like no woman ever loved a man."

He gasped, fought his way through a troubled fog then broke out into the bright light of understanding. His eyes softened and seemed to melt over her making her heart ache. "Well ... what do you know! This place, you and him together all the time ... and you're the loveliest woman I ever saw. I'm glad ... He's suffered so."

Her eyes grew wet in the light of his understanding. "Yes, I know. I hope he never suffers again, and Tommy ..."

"Yes?"

"Thanks an awful lot. Some day you may come to know what it meant to me to see how you took the news." She took his face in her slender hands and kissed him like the heart of a red rose, in the mouth and disappeared.

He stood transfixed by a number of emotions then walked dazedly through to the back and on out where the long red hogs rotted contentedly in their pen.

On the veranda Ronald let go a dry mirthless chuckle. "When I was his age I would react exactly as he has yet when you said we'd pull up I almost applauded. Of course, we'll do no such thing. I'm glad you didn't pull the 'offended father who is doing what is best' act and really burn the meat."

Berry sighed. "Did you see the boy? Hell, he'd have taken on a small army single handedly."

"I thrilled for him, I envied him, and for a flash of a second I hated him."

Berry's glance was compassionate. "It's got you bad hasn't it, boy?"

"It's got me. Yet I have another small victory to add to my almost non-existant store. I did follow him when I was morally certain there'd be trouble. At least I didn't break and run although I must admit I wanted to the worst way."

"There's another thing, Ron. Who knows what we'll do about it, but something ... No I don't mean that because the act of *doing* something of this sort is always silly. I mean about Ferris and Tommy."

Ron recoiled inwardly. Here was another matter he let his mind dwell upon very little. Necessarily so. "What chance do I stand against him," he said bitterly. "He's youth and bounce and romance. What am I? A burned out husk fit for the bone yard. Afraid of my shadow and loaded with all sorts of crossed purposes. I freeze up when I'm around her because she's a little too direct for me ... all this when I should be making time. What will he do about being run off the place? He isn't the sort to take something like that lying down."

"I've been meaning to pay that gentleman a visit but that'd look silly, too. He could shoot me for trespassing."

"He wouldn't do that but what could you gain?"

"That's the point. Nothing'd be gained and I'd be made to look pretty silly."

"Maybe Tommy's a little smarter than you or I. I think we're pushing things to bother about that now."

"That's what I said. But what do you feel about the business?"

Ronald emitted a rough, haw! "What can I do except sit here and watch. I'm damn sure not going to tell him to lay off. That'd make me sillier than you bracing Macklin. I'm going to sit and watch."

"And do nothing," snapped Berry short temperedly. "While you're doing nothing he'll be making hay and carrying her off on a white charger. Then maybe he'll meet some other little cute chick and dump Ferris like a hot potato. Youth works that way you know."

"That's a dismal picture you present. I wouldn't want her hurt."

"Yeah, but you don't want it strong enough to do anything objective about it like marrying her."

"I'm too old," said Ronald weakly.

"You're an ass," said Berry violently. "I'll bet you don't even know how old she is."

"Not a day over seventeen."

"Several, bud. She's twenty. She's been held down and under-fed until she doesn't look old. Her speech is tops because she's had a pretty good informal education and an appetite for books. She reasons like a mathematician because she has that sort of mind. She plays the piano like no one I ever heard. I've heard masters whose techniques were flawless, mechanically without peers, and every note was true and in place. She's different and not mechanical. She manages to get more of herself into her music than anyone I ever saw. Getting someone like Ferris into a song could certainly do no less than immortalize it."

Ronald managed a laugh. "Every man around here thinks a little too much of every woman around here."

"No variation of opinion," said Berry with a grin. "Well, I think a lot of Ferris but it's fatherly and on the rest you can count me out."

"That's a crock of Scandinavian ..."

Berry's rejoinder was too quick. "What the hell are you talking about now?"

Ronald nodded. "Sure, jump down my throat and make a certainty of it."

"What do you mean? And come out with it or I'll choke you."

"Are you sure you want me to?"

"No," said Berry after a pause. "Let it go."

"But you're not admitting it?"

"I don't have to and shut up will you?"

"I will because you're bigger 'n me. Just don't kid yourself. You're too old for things like that."

There was another long pause then Berry asked. "How did you know?"

"She told me."

"Oh, no."

"Yeah ... I've come out with smiliar brilliant retorts here of late."

Berry sighed. "Somehow I feel better."

"I should think so. You must have done quite some wrestling with yourself, swearing in a loud mental voice that it wasn't so."

"Something like that. It was the day I kicked Bud Kitchen off the place. It hit me and I hid it fast."

"Not fast enough. So ... Now what?"

"I don't know."

"Well, she'll let it go so far then something'll happen."

"Like what?"

"Come boy, surely you don't need a picture drawn." Instantly he remembered when he needed one before he could see.

"I know but I don't like that somehow. Shady dealings, no chance to make things right. Sort of dirty."

"She doesn't feel that way about it. I gathered that she was willing to go around the codes and laws if she couldn't change them ... and of course she can't and neither can you. She seems to feel that what she couldn't help or change she could beat in her own way. The legal angle you're worried about is a hangover from your rearing."

"It's the looks of the thing," said Berry grinding his hands together. "She deserves something better."

"Will she ever get it?"

"As to that I couldn't say. She could marry some good man of her own race ..."

Ronald laughed sardonically. "What is her race?"

"Well, she could find a man who is in the same boat she's in."

"I don't know whether she could or not. Think about it a little and you'll see that there'd have to be a lot of conditions satisfied. Then the one thing you haven't thought of is, maybe she wants it this way."

"Brother," Berry breathed, "but that Johnny's a prophet."

"He's a good cook too," added Ronald inconsequentially.

Berry massaged his face hard. "Things are happening around here with a rapidity that make them slightly unbelievable. The day we stepped off the train a damn twister tore through the town, people were killed, the church burned, we saw a ghoul taking a baby around to show the stick driven in its head. Tommy lurches in on us and today he killed a man. Somehow it's unreal. My son, a bare kid, just twenty-one, knocked off a human being and we sit here and gab as though nothing has happened."

"I don't see why we should be more concerned than he is."

"Well, I'm wondering about that. He's fired up with the spirit of battle and who knows what he might run into."

"He might but if he does and isn't shot in the back I'm thinking he'll give a good account of himself."

CHAPTER TWELVE

"I," announced Tommy as he shoved his chair back from the table, "am going to squire a lovely girl to a night of fun, frolic and wassail."

"Who's the poor creature," asked his father.

"The inimitable Ferris, who else? You know, that gal's sprouting like a watered plant. I'll bet she's gained seven pounds since I've been here."

"She eats something once in a while," said Berry. "She's been half starved by that old fanatic of a father. How do you intend to outfit him?"

Tommy's eyes narrowed. "There isn't but one way as far as I can see. Take her anyway. She'll be over after a while. He probably won't even miss her."

Ronald, having taken all he could of this conversation, got up abruptly and walked away.

"What's the matter with him," Tommy wanted to know.

Berry thought for a moment then decided against the impulse that nagged at him. "Who knows? Your Uncle Ron is in a pretty bad shape but I think he'll be all right eventually."

Tommy frowned. "I've heard rumors and stuff that he cracked up in Korea but I never heard the straight dope."

"What you heard was about the substance of it. He'll probably tell you all about it some day. Until then let it go. Never mention it to him."

"Oh ... I wouldn't think of it. I was just wondering."

Unker Ben sat on the bottom step of the porch and looked moodily at the rampant colors of the sunset. The beauty of the moment did not reach him because he was wrestling with a problem that had been placed in his mind by Ronald Summerville. Could Ferris be Sally? He shook his head. Although they were as alike as peas in a pod, Sally couldn't be as young as Ferris. Some folks said that Sally was dead but if she was why couldn't he remember the funeral? Ferris came out of the house in a very simple white dress. Her lips were touched with a bit of forbidden lipstick but she wore no other cosmetics. Unker Ben, especially clear of mind this afternoon, felt his ancient heart leap at the sight of her. If in truth Sally was dead, might it not be possible that she had come back in the form of Ferris?

He had never met Ferris' mother so he didn't know what she looked like. At this moment Ferris was an angel. Her gunmetal hair had been parted in the middle and now bounced in two pony tails tied with red ribbons. Her lips were lushly scarlet, her cheeks pink and her eyes huge and starry. Sally had always liked white, he remembered, and wore it a great deal.

Unker Ben had a great idea. As she came nearer, smiling at him for the world like Sally he said, "Evenin' Sally."

The girl's face froze for a fraction of a second then lighted again. Her voice was low and soft as she spoke. "Good evening, Ben."

She didn't stop however, and went on toward the bluff, disappearing finally down the path toward the Summervilles'.

Unker Ben's chest heaved painfully and his long dry eyes flooded with tears. "Sally," he murmured softly as she disappeared down the part toward the Summervilles'. "Sally."

CHAPTER THIRTEEN

Ronald Summerville was drunk but for the first time in years he was happily drunk.

Ronald's happiness was effectively squelched when he heard the car drive into the garage.

He got up abruptly and went out onto the front lawn and wandered aimlessly until he thought they had had plenty of time to finish with their goodbyes, then he started back toward the house and almost stumbled over them. Tommy was holding her close. "But I want to go home with you. You shouldn't be walking through these woods alone."

"No," she said positively. "It's an imposition and I'm afraid he might see you. Good night Tommy."

"That's not a very good good night." Her face turned up to his in question but she never voiced it.

His lips closed over hers and for a long moment they clung, her body in hard resistance but her lips avid and eager. Finally she drew gently away. "That was very nice Tommy ... but you shouldn't have done it." Ronald stumbling away as fast as he could, running, did not hear the last sentence.

After breakfast the next morning there was a staff meeting. The matter of last night had been discussed thoroughly and Tommy, high in the brass because of his exploits, was a little too high to be effectually squelched.

"I say that if this is the way these people play around here, why do we sit here like ducks in a rain barrel? They're the ones on the offensive and that leaves us to take countermeasures. Why don't we make them take some counter measures?"

Berry who was turning the problem of his belligerent son over in his mind as rapidly as he could and still expect the effort to bear fruit sighed thunderously. "Tommy, why do you think we have the support of the law in this matter?"

Tommy opened his mouth for a quick retort, realized that in its very speed might lurk error, closed it again and fell silent.

"I'll tell you. It's because we're the ones who have been on the defensive. The moment we go on the prod, then we become one of the other side. As long as we stay on the side of the law we are safe from that angle. We can't go riding for the Kitchens. We'll just have to sit and hope."

Tommy nodded slowly. "I guess I hadn't thought of that. I suppose you're right but I'm telling you from now on, I'm shooting at the first shadow I see on the place."

"And" said Ronald sardonically, "it'll probably turn out to be me."

Tommy stared. "In that case, Uncle Ron, suppose you knock off your wandering till this this is over."

"And that" said Berry, "contains the elements of good advice. I'm on the verge of trigger happiness myself."

That broke up the caucus, that and the fact that the Marks boys had reported a break in the fence close enough to the highway as to constitute a hazard to wandering stock. Also there was the matter of a cow who seemed to be having trouble with calf-birth.

Ronald, paced up and down for a long time, relived the scene of last night and almost perished from acute misery.

When the phone rang he jumped as though one of the Kitchen's had taken a pot shot at him. He stood for a moment, his face damp with sweat then like a man conquering some palpable enemy he lifted the receiver.

"Hello."

"Ron." The bells again, ranks of them all blended into one soothing honey smooth note.

"Oh ... Carla. Something the matter?"

"Why would I be calling you if there was? I have a day off. Does that suggest anything to you?"

His heart leaped powerfully and he became weak. He sat shakily in a chair, his mind racing over the camp house and Carla, her fair white skin and the ravening cannibalism of her lush lips.

"Well ..."

"Good, say in an hour? I have hot dogs, Coke and everything all packed with ice in a camp cold box. Both my brothers are in Jackson for two days."

"In an hour" he said weakly.

Carla was dressed in an off white sports outfit that consisted of a skirt, a pair of shorts and a sleeveless jacket that missed meeting the skirt by some inches, revealing a surcingle of delightful satiny skin. The skirt buttoned up the front, but only two buttons were being used and her round exciting thighs peeped through as she walked. He carried the box with the ice and drinks while she carried the weiners, rolls and a few jars of different spreads.

They stowed the picnic in the trunk of the car and got in.

"Either button that dress or drive" he said with a grin. "I'll make us wreck."

She smiled and skidded further out of the dress. "Do you like my legs, Ron?"

"They're sumptuous."

"You make them sound fat."

"Well, they aren't fat, they're just sufficient. Nothing spindly or weak in their architecture."

"Thank you, sir." They were on the main street of town but that did not stop her from leaning over and kissing him explosively over the ear.

"Stop it. What'll the neighbors say?"

"They're calling me Mrs. Summerville already."

"I apologize. It must be one of the many worms that eat on me. You saw how quickly I accepted, didn't you?"

"That took some of the sting from my pride. Are you really glad I called?"

"You'll never know. I was walking up and down nearly ready to scream."

"See that tree half a mile down the road?"

"Sure, you mean that big gum?"

"Yes. That's where you first kissed me. I want to be kissed again beneath that tree."

He kissed her again and, as before, the world whirled dizzily, and he felt like a man going under ether for the first time. She was soft-hard, eager and as pliant as a reed. Her lips were live passionate messengers with an edict to deliver.

Finally she drew back. "Let's ride, Ron ... fast."

They rode swiftly and before many minutes elapsed he turned off the highway onto the graveled one, then later onto the weed grown path that led to the camp.

They unloaded the car, interrupting the procedure for a long kiss beneath the trees, finished and sat for a while on the camp porch facing the gurgling river, drinking tall icy drinks.

The day had been idyllic. She was a golden white goddess whose limbs were wonders, whose breasts were inverted cups of honey and whose love was strong and consistent. They had loved, and eaten and bathed in the river and were now sprawled out on the big hooked rug in front of the fireplace wherein flickered a tiny flame.

She rolled over on her stomach, head chin in hands, her full breasts telescoping back and spreading at their bases in a manner that contracted his muscles involuntarily.

"How have things progressed?" she asked. "I mean are you still convinced that you're a coward."

He nodded miserably.

She frowned. "Let me tell you a few things about yourself. First, those little victories must have meant something deep down because if they hadn't you wouldn't have remembered them. Second, I don't like this habit you have of making small of something your subconscious must have thought was enough of a victory to make you hoard them."

"Your logic" he said with a sad smile, "is unassailable, but the facts remain. Logic for some reason fails to reach the trigger."

He chuckled. "Two women in my life have meant a great deal to me on the positive side. Another one has meant a great deal on the negative side. Every time I get near the frazzled edge one or the other of you comes to my aid and all is well."

Her laugh was genuine. "It's a good thing I'm me or I'd hate you for saying that there's another woman."

"There isn't really. You'd never feel jealous of her. She used her treatment just as a doctor would use terramycin. Actually, she's in love with my brother. I think she does it because she knows that our welfare is rather entangled, one with the other. I think if Tommy needed her, she'd not hesitate a moment."

"I think," she said looking up at him, "that you mean something more than physical need."

"I do. Physical relief is an anodyne for many obscure conditions. I heard a man say once that a woman was more vulnerable when she was in the gloom of grief than at any other time."

"There's some truth to that, I think."

"I think so too ..." His eyes found hers and held for a moment. With a leap she was in his arms and their breaths whistled with the urgence of respiration.

The door slammed loudly and Alex Kitchen stood watching them, his eyes and face red from the drinks he had been taking along the way. He watched until their consciousness was of the kind that can admit environmental impressions. Carla saw him first and tore herself from Ronald's palsied clutch with a muffled scream and cowered back against a divan. Ronald turned over and his stomach congealed into a leaden icy lump of terror.

"Pretty," snarled Alex, his gun carelessly on them. "Very pretty." He looked the girl over with hot lecherous eyes until she blushed from the heat of his gaze. "Ummm. Prettier yet. Blush again babe. I didn't know people blushed any place except their faces. Well, you learn something every day. Get up Summerville. Where do you want it? In the head, in the belly? You name it."

Carla started forward, a half scream on her lips only to be gestured back by the muzzle of the .45.

"Stay put, girlie" he said with a leer. "I'll get to you later, after I deal with this yankee. What's the matter, Summerville, cat got your tongue?"

Ronald's entire body was icy cold, but he did manage to stand up and lean against the table that held his clothes. His throat worked but no words came.

Alex laughed gratingly. "Madelyn was right, you're as yellow as an alley cat. Still can't talk? Better try, cause I'm likely to pick my own place." The thought of what this man's family had done to the proud name of Kitchen and red rage flared anew in his brain. He raised the gun snicking the big hammer back in audible clicks. "If this don't teach them relatives of yourn what it means to tangle with the Kitchens then we got something for them, too."

A thought occurred to him and he grinned. "I got a better idea." He looked at the nude figure of Carla and said, "Come here, baby."

Like a sleepwalker she came slowly toward him, her face dead and her eyes glazed with terror.

"Nope, better not. Sonny boy might try to jump us here. Let's have fun on that sofa over there, that'll give me time to bring him down if he tries to jump us."

He led her across the big room where the door led to the kitchen and threw her on the divan and placed his gun carefully on the arm of it. Then he slowly disrobed, a hateful grin on his red face.

Ronald felt like he was seeing a movie through the wrong end of a telescope. His body was still as cold as a block of ice and as stiff. Horror mounted in him until it seemed it would blot out his consciousness. Alex sat on the sofa beside her and let his thick rough hands wander over her breasts and stomach. Carla stiffened, half sat up, a low moan of hysteria rising in her throat, then she collapsed in a faint.

Ronald wondered long afterward what it was that caused it to happen, but was never able to put his finger on any one detail of the grisly scene. All he knew that suddenly, like a light going on, fear fled, and hot fierce blood coursed through his veins. Rage hovered over his head like a pall of crimson, but his eyes and mind were crystal clear and a course plain before him.

Under his shirt was his pistol and smoothly and without haste he flipped the garment off the table and picked up the weapon.

"Get up, Alex."

142

SPLENDORS OF LOVE

If he had been prodded in a tender place with a white hot iron the big man could not have started more violently. He got up and Ronald watched the blood drain from the surface of his skin leaving it splotched with bluish pigment.

Ronald still stood with one hand on the table, leaning on it slightly. Now he turned and walked around, placing his back to it. "Alex get your gun."

"No" the other whispered harshly. "You'd shoot me."

"That's right, I will. You were going to shoot me ... remember?"

"I was just bluffin' you."

"I'm not bluffing. Get the gun and you'll have a chance."

Alex's thick body with it's thick shag of red hair tensed and his eyes narrowed. His stomach labored with heavy shuddery breathing and like a flash he dived for the gun. Ronald then did a very foolish thing. Like lightning the thought flashed through his head and with his old devil may care attitude he put it into effect. *He'll miss that first shot.*

He let the big gun swing around and a split second after the flash he fired. A small blue hole appeared in Alex's upper abdomen. Ronald walked closer, Again he fired ... and another hole joined the first very close. Still the big man did not fall. He bent over clutching his stomach which now began to spill thick blood that worked its way between the clutching fingers. Ronald, as cool as a man on a firing range aimed deliberately ... and missed cleanly. He stopped and lowered the gun. He was no murderer and this was murder. Alex began to reel and finally crashed so hard to the floor that he bounced.

Ronald felt his pulse and though it was fluttery from shock it still beat.

"Oh Ron ..." Carla was sitting up now. "That was the nerviest or stupidest thing I ever saw."

"What?"

"Letting him come all the way around with that gun. You could have shot him easily before he even got his hands on it. You gave him first shot, deliberately."

"Get your clothes on darling. It's hard to hit a man swinging around like that. Didn't you mention once that this place had a phone?"

"Yes. It's in the kitchen."

CHAPTER FOURTEEN

For supper that night Johnny completely outdid himself. They had restocked the deep freeze that day and Ronald had never seen such magnificent T-bones. He had brought Carla home with him for a number of reasons, some of which he would not have admitted even to himself. Charley stayed and partook of the feast of charcoal broiled steaks, cooked out of doors in the barbecue pit. There was a long rustic table set with flowers and stacked with delicious food. Tender crisp green celery, ripe and green olives, tomatoes, green onions, sweet peppers and quartered lettuce reposed in an immense scarlet bowl filled with chipped ice. There was a big bowl of orange colored sauce that gave off a delightful fragrance in which to dip the salad vegetables ... a strictly hand to mouth business. Long french bread smothered in butter and garlic sat in ranks in two wicker baskets and there were several bottles of sparkling Burgundy squatting in ice pails.

"What's the idea" asked Ronald of Berry.

"I think Mart thought it up and Johnny carried it out. Not a bad idea. Perfect night for it."

Ronald and Charley had decided it best to wait until morning to tell of the day's activities so there had been no mention of the trouble.

Ferris was present, hovered over by Tommy until he had to divide his attentions between the two girls when Ronald went in to shave. Berry had gone with him. "What the hell gives? I haven't seen you look this way in years." All he got was an enigmatic smile and a promise of a story the next day and with that he had to be content.

The meal was a big success ... or so it seemed to Ronald although he did notice Tommy squirming trying to divide his attention equally between the two girls.

When the meal was over Ronald announced his intention to take Carla home because her mother might be worried and they left.

Carla sat quietly for half a mile then said. "Your nephew is nice."

"Hell of a good kid. The best."

"He was quite attentive remembering that he already had a girl there."

"I noticed that."

"Was that all you noticed, Ron?"

"What do you mean?"

"Ferris, who by the way is a really beautiful girl, pecked at her food and hardly took her eyes off you."

"No," Ron could feel his face getting hot. "No, I didn't notice that."

"It's a wonder her eyes didn't burn your back when we started to the car. They burned me, I know. Ron, she's in love with you."

He sighed. "Hell, Tommy's in love with her."

"Well, I can tell you it isn't Tommy she loves. How do you feel about her?"

It took him a while to think of a good answer to that and when he did he discovered it to be the most direct one he could think of. "I'm in love with her, Carla."

She reached over and touched his hand. "I'm glad you could be straight about it like that. I'm glad you know me well enough to know you don't have to flower anything up just because of what's gone on between us. I've enjoyed us a great deal, Ron and

I'm never going to let anything come between me and what has been the two most wonderful dates I can imagine. If you love her then you love her and that's that."

"They threw the pattern away when they made you," he said huskily. "If I may be allowed a momentary triteness."

"Ron, will you do something for me?"

"Certainly, what?"

"You know where the old dipping vat is, up about five hundred yards?"

"Yes."

"Pull in there and hide us good."

He pulled in beside the rotting old pens and the vat with its rusty tin roof ... further until a clump of thick gum trees effectively hid them from the road, and stopped.

Her face was a shadow close to his, hanging in the dim light like a wraith of all loveliness, a dim white patch against a background of purple night. Her hands touched his face with a gentleness that made his heart ache. "Ron, this may be the last time. Make me remember it like the other two."

Her lips enveloped his and although feeling that his admission of love for Ferris had placed him beyond the pale and therefore should not react as he had before that same flickering nerve-shredding shock coursed through his body and a hungry sound came from his throat.

"Good mornin', God" Unker Ben let his eyes slide a little to the northwest and saw the anvil head of a thunder cloud pink in the morning sunrise. "Thunder 'fore seven, rain 'fore 'leven," he murmured quoting an old saying to do with the weather. "'Scuse me ... just seen that thunder head over there and kinda thought maybe it'd rain. Ain't had no rain in some time and thought maybe you'd turn loose and let it rain. Bet you're lettin' it rain some place in the sea where it's already wet as hell. But like the parson says, you ain't in the habit of 'splainin' things to people". He stopped and frowned thoughtful. "Sumpn else I had on my mind ... Oh, that there Summerville boy mentioned t' other day that Ferris might be Sally. Now I know good's anybody that Ferris ain't Sally. People been tellin' me for a long time Sally's dead but looks like if you had her, you'd let me know it. Or if you ain't got her and let 'er come back in Ferris ... well, maybe that's how come you ain't got her." He took out half a plug of tobacco and his natural generosity tempted him to offer God a chew but the matter of protocol intervened.

"Ferris is Sally," came a voice. *"In my wisdom I placed her in your house and you did not understand."*

Unker Ben reeled away from the lip of the bluff, his face twisted with fear and almost blue. Swiftly he looked around but at that moment the only new thing to be seen was the new sun just clearing the pines on the eastern horizon.

"Go home, Ben, and grieve for Sally no more. She has spoken to me as loyally as you have and she still loves you, just as you remember. Even, more, perhaps, because you would not believe her dead."

For a long time Unker Ben remained stiff as a block of stone, but God spoke no more. He turned slowly and with many a backward glance walked toward the house.

Ferris came to meet him and opened the yard gate. "Unker Ben, you came back early."

He came close and studied her like she was someone new and intriguing. "Sure," he whispered, his eyes flooding with tears. "Sure you're her ... ain't you?"

She looked at him perplexed for a moment then she remembered the faded old picture of Sally and how greatly she resembled her. Ferris' breast ached fiercely and her mind raced furiously to try to decide the correct thing to say.

"Yes," she whispered. "Yes."

"Knowed it … Nup. Mustn't tell a lie. Young Summerville told me, then I asked God."

A trembling smile touched her face. "And what did God say?"

The rheumy old eyes fastened to hers with a grip of iron. "I'll tell you cause if you're really her, then you'll understand me and won't think I'm lyin'."

"Unker Ben, you wouldn't lie to me."

" 'Course I wouldn't … Be more fitten for you just to call me plain Ben, wouldn't it?"

"All right, Ben. What did He tell you?"

"My memory ain't what it uster was," he said profoundly, "but I'll never forget them words. 'Ferris is Sally,' plain's day He said it. Yes, sir, and that ain't all He said."

Sam Williams and Charley Olsen came out that day about eight o'clock and sat on the front veranda drinking small cups of powerful pungent coffee that Berry and Ronald now liked.

"Well," said Sam putting his cup down. "Tommy got one and Ron got one. When you gonna get yours, Berry?"

"I hope I don't have to get any, Sam. What's Alex's condition this morning?"

"Holding on. Second bullet cut the lobe of the right lung and the first one spilled grits and gravy and sowbelly all over his abd … er, belly cavity. Ten years ago he'd been a goner but the way they got things now he might pull through. How come you didn't shoot him again, Ron?"

Ronald grimaced. "Because he was down with two holes in him. I don't shoot a man to bits for the love of it."

"Well, I hope it don't never come back to you. He'd a shot you till his ammunition give out."

Charley said, "Well, I can see Ron's side of that set up. Just like shooting a man when he's unarmed. Ron let him get his gun and fire the first shot."

"And," said the sheriff positively, "that was a mistake, too."

"Hindsight," grunted Charley, "comes easy. He acted according to his lights."

"Come out to tell you," said Sam as he placed his cup on the stone flagging, "that Sim Ellerson, foreman of the Grand Jury, took a quick poll of the members and they ain't even gonna bring you in. Turned out that the District Attorney is fed up with the Kitchens and he didn't open his mouth one way or 'nother. He knowed he couldn't get a conviction. Same thing for Alex. Plain case of him goin' after Ron."

"Well, that's a relief," said Berry, "eh, Tommy?"

Tommy started and looked up. "Er ... sure, Pop. When do we go?"

They all looked at him at once making him blush. "Son of a gun" commented Sam, "he didn't even hear what I said."

When they had gone Tommy cornered Ronald and after much wriggling and stumbling managed to get what was troubling him out into the open. "Uncle Ron, that girl you brought here last night ... What I mean is ... Are you in love with her?" He brought it out with a rush.

There was a strange heavenly weakness in the pit of Ronald's stomach. "What about Ferris?"

"Ferris? Well, Ferris ... " He stumbled and stopped looking anywhere but into his uncle's eyes. "Ferris ... You want to know about Ferris. Well, she's a swell girl. Cute too."

"Playing the field?"

Tommy wriggled with discomfort. "No sir ... I know what it sounds like. I thought I was in love with her until last night."

"And now you're in love with Carla?"

Tommy smiled weakly. "Sounds silly, doesn't it?"

"Does it?"

"All I know is that when that Carla girl looked at me last night, I went in over my head. I had to strain so as not to leave Ferris out of things completely. All right ... maybe I'm fickle. I never had anyone to trip me like Carla, though."

"What'll you tell Ferris?"

Tommy cringed. "Do you reckon you could sort of hint around that I think she's a swell girl and all that but ... You'll know what to say."

"Nope. Do your own communication. If I have much dealing with Ferris I'll wind up married to her."

Tommy's eyes went blank. "You ... ?"

Ronald's spirits soared. He could talk about it now but before he hardly dared think of it. "Yes, me. All the while you were daddling around here looking goo-goo eyes at her I could have strangled you. All I hope is that she'll consider it good riddance." He grinned. "Good hunting, Casanova."

Ham Jones was small, black and frightened but he had a mission to fulfill.

After the indicated amount of snooping and no little belly crawling, Ham saw Ferris Macklin start out from the rear of the house dressed as she liked when walking, in faded tattered blue shorts and an old grey shirt with the tail tied high under her high breasts.

He took off his cap and stepped into the path, confronting her. "Evenin', Miss."

"Good evening. Did you want to see someone?"

"Yessum, I got a note fer you."

She took it, opened it and read it carefully, color mounting to her cheeks and her breath coming faster. She folded it and tucked it into her shirt pocket. 'Thank you. There won't be any answer."

Ham, his mission finished, of which he knew almost nothing, walked through the woods until he came to his mule, mounted and took a little path that would take him to the highway where the road turned off to the Summerville House. It was no surprise therefore, when he saw one of the Summerville gentlemen, walking toward him.

He pulled his mule respectfully aside and waited so Ronald could pass. Ronald stopped and eyed the boy suspiciously. "Where've you been, boy?"

Ham smiled ingratiatingly, exposing large white teeth that shone from the very black background of his face. "I been t' d'liver a note."

"Note? To whom?"

Ham had had no instructions as to his conduct should he meet anyone else and besides white people's business was their business and beyond what was directly ordered he did not trespass. "Miss Ferris Macklin."

Swiftly, Ronald pictured the woods between the Summerville tract and the Macklin's. There was no line fence to amount to anything. Macklin had no cattle and cattle from the Summerville plantation had always roamed freely there. In return, Berry saw to it that the line fences of the Macklin's where they adjoined other places were kept in order. The boy wouldn't have had any trouble getting from Little River Plantation where he was now to the Macklin house. But what was he doing on Little River and who had written the note? "Who sent the note?"

Promptly and without the slightest misgivings Ham said, "Well, we was over on Mis Potter's place and Mr. Bud Kitchen tole me t' bring a note to Miss Ferris ..." That was as far as he got.

Ronald turned, burst through the underbrush like an elephant, and was gone.

Ham sat on his mule and scratched his head ... then it came to him ... things he had hardly listened to. First, because it was none of his business. Second, because it was white people's business and there had been some shooting His face turned greyish and he urged the mule into a trot then a back breaking gallop. He had overtalked himself, he had given away some strategy that although vague in his mind, he felt mortally certain was not vague in the mind of Bud Kitchen ... or Ronald Summerville.

The sun was sinking low and turning the world a soft dusty crimson. Unker Ben sat on the front steps, his eyes on the black masses of clouds, his old heart drumming happily if somewhat rustily. He looked at the clouds but did not see them. All he could see was the laughing eyes of Sally, the new and younger Sally.

The figure of a running man caught his eye from an angle and with a feeling of irritation he turned and watched Ronald Summerville sprinting at top speed toward the house. He tore open the gate and stopped breathlessly in front of Unker Ben. "Where's Ferris?"

Unker Ben smiled understandingly. Now that he could see who it was he remembered that this young man had not only helped him search for Sally but had even suggested that Ferris might be her. He felt warmly about it and inclined to be obliging. "Sally, you mean. Well, you know Sally. She's probably off in the woods ramblin' some place. You was right, young man ... she *is* Sally."

Ronald almost tore his hair with impatience. "Unker Ben ... where? You don't have any idea where she went?"

"No, son, I don't. You look all fired upset over sumpn."

Ronald leaned close. "Bud Kitchen sent her a note to meet him ... only he probably signed someone else's name to it.

Understand me, Unker Ben? And you know Bud Kitchen. He tried to rape her twice."

Unker Ben snapped suddenly erect. "Now by God, kissin' is one thing, Hamp Jackson ..." He got to his feet, his eyes glittering feverishly, "but ravishin', that's another." He frowned. Who was it that had come inside where he was watching girls duck for apples and told him Sally was having trouble with Hamp? Oh, Bill Stevens. Well, who mentioned ravishment? Was it Dunc Pearson? Might have been. Some young man that was sure upset about something. Didn't matter who it was.

With the spring of a young man Unker Ben went up the steps and saw Dowd standing in the door.

"Where is that ungrateful girl? Do you know I haven't had supper yet?"

"Who gives a durn" said Unker Ben harshly. "Sally's about to get ravished and you talk about supper. Go graze in that there garden 'mongst all that grass you raises."

"Wasn't that that unregenerate hellion Summerville you were talking to?"

"Nope, that was Bill Stevens. Now outa my way. I got things to do."

He went to his room and from over the mantle piece where it had hung for a long time he took a single barrel shotgun.

He took out several old shotgun shells with long brass bases.

He stood for a moment on the back porch, aware of a curious stuffiness in his chest but he attributed it to excitement. He peered into the woods that were darkening now, and pondered. Where had Dunc said she was? He didn't say, he asked me. Funny. If he knew so much how come he had to ask? Well, she used to love to swim in the creek on Little River Plantation.

CHAPTER FIFTEEN

art, answering the strident summons of the telephone bell, lifted the receiver. "Hello."

"Is Mr. Berry Summerville there," asked a thick unsteady woman's voice.

"No ma'm."

"Is Tommy there?"

"No ma'm he isn't here either."

"Well, now isn't that just wonderful. How very considerate they are. It would have been inconvenient if they had been. All right, my golden skinned chippie, tell Mr. Ronald that if he wants to save his little Ferris from a fate worse than death he'd better get down to the swimming hole on the creek."

The receiver at the other end crashed and Mart leaned against the wall, sick with dread. She remembered Ronald springing across the lawn not ten minutes ago ... he must know and he was headed straight for a trap. She remained slumped leaning against the wall for a moment then her head came up. *"Johnny?"*

"Damn," he muttered coming to the door rubbing his left hand with a dish towel. "You made me spill hot grease on myself. What on earth ..."

She told him in a few swift words, "Now listen to me. You've called me hard-headed but I've been as soft as an egg compared to now. Doesn't Mr. Berry have a shotgun?"

"Yes, an automatic."

"Get it and load it. Put more shells in your pocket. I think Mr. Ronald's pistol's in his room. I'll take that. We're in this family for better or worse. So far it's been a snap. *Now move.*"

Ronald hadn't run so far so fast since Korea when he fled the battle lines in mad hysterical fear and his lungs seemed on fire when he came to the flat land bordering the creek. On he plunged, calling to her at the top of his voice. He plunged through a fringe of elder bushes and all went black.

Thunder battered at his ears and he could feel the wind rising and tugging at his clothes.

"Coming to," said a voice that he didn't recognize.

"Ferris is makin' out she's still fainted," said a voice he recognized as Bud's. "Better run on in to town and make that call t' get that boy and Berry Summerville down here. Slim and Mose and Luke get here yet?"

"They're down at the road waiting."

"Okay, go ahead. I can take care of the situation now. Tell them boys to come on up here and take their positions. I'll spot 'em so they can get Summerville and his boy."

Ronald with a superhuman effort rolled over and sat up. His hands and feet were securely tied and his head banged like the hammer of Thor was seeking entry. Twilight was still lingering because the sunset still glowed in the west. Before him, sprawled in loose limbed grace was Ferris. Her feet were tied but her hands weren't.

"Well," grated Bud taking a drink from a bottle. "Look who's woke up."

Ronald tried to think of something crushing to say but fear rode him too heavily. Not fear for himself this time, but fear for the girl.

Grinning Bud walked over and rolling her over ripped the shirt from her with a single powerful wrench. "Ummm," he gloated. "Boy, looka there." He caught her to him and mouthed her silken skin with his thick loose lips, letting them wander to the rose tinted tips of her breasts. Ronald broke out with cold sweat and his head reeled as did his stomach. Bud caught the girl's shorts in his hands and ripped them away with cruel strength.

"Hey, Summerville, don't it make your mouth water, boy? Don't you wish you was me now?"

"What would a hero of mine say now?" Ronald asked himself. "How would he get out of these ropes and charge an armed man?" Ronald's head hung in numb abject defeat. There was no moving of the ropes. There was no hope. Bud would take her before his eyes and as long as he lived the horror of the act would live with him. He'd hurt her because he didn't care. He'd brutalize her slim lovely body with his obscene carcass. His big sweaty red body would stiffen and writhe in passion ... He strained until his ears popped and sang crazily. Lightning tore across the sky and thunder rolled but he neither saw nor heard.

Ferris woke and screamed. It ripped into his nerves like the jagged edges of glass stands. In frantic fury he wrenched again at the ropes binding him but to no avail, save that now warm blood ran down his wrists into his hands.

She screamed again before Bud could clap a hand over her mouth but she fought with all the steel muscled fury of a leopard and Bud was having his hands full. He slammed her with his open hand and stunned her momentarily. In that moment he got the advantage he sought, and his heavy body pinned hers to the ground. "Now," he growled hoarsely, "You little hell cat ... you lookin,' Summerville?"

"We is," said Slim Kitchen as he and his two brothers walked up. "Go on, Bud. Give it to her good. Then us, hunh?"

"No …" He turned his head. "Y'all go on up the hill a ways and spread out cause some more's comin' and we're sweepin' clean tonight."

They left with many a backward glance and Bud grinned at Ronald. "Ready there, spectator? Damn, she fainted again."

Then like an apparition, Unker Ben was standing not ten feet away, his ancient eyes ablaze. "Hamp, get offen 'er."

Bud did a pushup, his face a blob of frozen surprise but Unker Ben was in no mood to waste words.

The old gun went off with like a small field piece and Bud's face seemed to dissolve in a welter of squirting blood. He rolled off the girl and scrambled around in the grass for a moment then stretched out and lay still, save for his hands that fluttered like the wings of a butterfly impaled on a pin.

"Unker Ben," gasped Ronald. "Cut us loose, for God's sake. There are others."

Unker Ben took his time but as soon as Ronald was free he snatched the gun. "Have any more shells?"

Unker Ben seemed to wilt and shrink as he fumbled with his pockets. "Couple, some place. Here."

"Watch Ferris," shouted Ronald over the thunder and wind.

With a bound he took off in the direction taken by the other three Kitchens.

A rifle cracked ahead of him only to be drowned out by the drum fire of a repeater shotgun fired with machine gun rapidity.

A scream of anguish flickered momentarily on the turbulent air like the flashes of lightning and following it came the crisp crash of an automatic pistol and a bullet snicked through the underbrush close to his head. Ronald hit the ground and began a fast crawl with the gun cradled in his crooked elbows.

He burst into an open glade and for a moment he was numb. Two men lay full length on the grass and across one of them lay Johnny, still clutching the shot gun. Locked with the slim boy Tommy had fought was Mart, and never in his life had Ronald been such insane ferocity displayed by a human being. Her pistol was gone, as was Slim's rifle, her clothes were nearly torn from her but she was far from defeated. Like a tigress gone mad, she ripped and tore at the tall boy. She was all over him, her long nails cutting like razor blades. His clothes were torn and he bled profusely from several bites where she had cut him like a wolf. Risking extinction, his hand went into his pocket and came out with a long switch blade knife which he snapped open.

Ronald yelled a warning and aimed his gun but they rolled and pitched with such fury that he was afraid to shoot. Suddenly, with a single herculean wrench that tore the knife from his hands and sent rippling muscles across her back and shoulders into tense definition, she changed the situation and with a movement two swift for the eye to follow, she whipped the knife up and buried it to the hilt in Slim's throat. His scream was cut to a hoarse bubbling croak, cut off like a switch had been thrown as she surged back with all her strength and ripped him open from jaw to ear. Blood spouted like water from a hose and spread a veil of gore over her superb body. Slowly she rose and with a final gesture of contempt hurled the knife at him. She wore the collar to her uniform, her shoes and a pair of skin tight briefs. All else had been torn from her. She stood for a moment like Diana over a kill, then fell to her knees and shuddered hard, sobs searing her throat fiercely.

He dropped on his knees beside her. "Are you hurt?"

"No ... please see about Johnny."

He got up and lifted Johnny off the body of Joe and turned him over. Blood flecked his lips and from a hole in his left chest a bubble rose and fell with his respiration.

At that moment Berry and Tommy burst through the bushes and stopped dead.

"Good lord, what's happened," asked Berry, his voice a hoarse rasp.

"What you see. Watch Johnny and Mart for a moment. She might go into hysterics …"

"*No,*" she sprang to her feet, dripping with blood, her fabulous breasts lifted and proud in spite of their gory surfaces. She was unashamed and now in control of herself. "Where did you leave Miss Ferris."

"Back there …"

"Then see to her. Don't mind us. We'll get Johnny back to the house."

Berry stood watching her and when a flash of lightning flared uttered a despairing croak.

"Good God, you're shot all to pieces."

"I'm not," she snapped back. "It's not my blood …" She swayed and he caught her in his arms, holding her close with savage strength. A soft moan dribbled from her lips and Tommy, his eyes glistening with moisture, turned away and began to examine Johnny.

Ferris was bending over Unker Ben who was seated against a tree. Her body glistened in the flashes of electric extravagance and on her silken skin ran the first few drops of the long threatened downpour.

"Are you all right, Sally?" He knelt beside her.

"I'm all right, but Unker Ben …"

The old man's hands were limp in his lap and his head lolled back against the trunk. His eyes were gradully dulling but on his dry wrinkled lips was a smile that seemed to cut into Ronald's vitals. "Sally," he whispered.

"Yes ... Ben."

"Did ... Hamp ... hurt ... you?"

"No, Ben. Not at all. You saved me."

The smile grew a little but his jaw seemed to slacken and fall. "Close the windows. Raining. Found Sally." The light in the old eyes went slowly dim, he gave a short quick gasp and his head dropped to one side.

"He's gone," she whispered.

Ronald tore at the clogging knot in his throat with an angry gruff. "Yes ... but he found Sally ... and he's smiling."

He gathered the old man into his arms and walked into the now pouring rain

Johnny had been shot clean through with a hard nosed bullet from an old .30-30 and was in no particular danger. He was getting the best attention that money could buy. Suddenly, for the first time in four years, Ronald felt the old familiar urge come over him. He had to get to a typewriter and tear into it with his old vim and speed. Again the tigerish form of Mart, her hair streaming wildly, serpentine muscles writhing under satin skin, the primordial ferocity of her attack and the steel strength with which she handled Slim Kitchen as though he were a child. He relived the chill horror of seeing the knife flash open and the lightning grab of her hand, the terrific power that she exerted, etching tendons on her skin like a fabulous bronze figurine, as she tore it from his grasp and the leaping plunge that sank it deep into his throat. He saw her teeth bared like a jungle animal as she exerted every ounce of her whalebone strength and ripped him open like a slaughtered beef. He passed a hand over his forehead. He must get it down ... and what would make a better setting for a story. Had they not all lived a story since the day when they were welcomed by the tornado?

He tossed and fretted a long time that night as the plot developed in his mind and kept him from sleep until at last exhaustion was served.

The next day was a busy one. The funeral, a meeting with the District Attorney at which he expressed sorrow at the trouble they had been caused and gave assurances that there would be no more.

They visited Johnny and found him cheerful and in as much comfort as a man with a hole in his chest might expect. They ate dinner with Charley Olsen and his wife which was an enormous spread and the good woman was overjoyed at the way they consumed her efforts.

They returned home early, mainly because Berry was fretting himself into a lather, the reason for which he did not mention but Ronald guessed and Tommy knew but offered no objection, as much as he wished to see Carla.

"Can I bring Carla to the wedding, Uncle Ron," he asked as they got out of the car?

"Of course ... I want everyone there who has had anything to do with all this mix up."

"By the way," said Berry, as they walked to the house. "Charley told me aside that Madelyn left for parts unknown this morning."

Ronald sighed. "Well ... happy days are here for sure."

It was dark and for the first time in ages Ronald felt so utterly at peace that it was like a drink of some potent soporific.

Ferris had refused to return to her home ... her first refusal. Her second had to do with the sleeping arrangement. At first she had refused to go to her own room, preferring to sit on the edge of his bed and drape herself like a delightful stole across his body.

He had insisted, so she went ... only to change to a shortie night-gown that was about as obscuring as a cigarette paper.

"God," he muttered as she stood in the doorway the dim light behind her providing a mouthwatering silhouette. "Ferris, it isn't a safe thing to do and the words haven't been spoken over us yet."

"I know," she said softly. "I'm afraid I'm not thinking about the words right now." She slid into bed with him and he could feel the excitement trembling and quaking through her velvet skin. Her mouth sought his and a thready little note crept from her throat telling of demand and the nearness of the limit of her resistance.

A long time later, at peace, seated and weary he held her close listening to the soft night sounds, the steady gradually slowing of her heartbeat and the easy sweet rhythm of her breathing.

THE END